SIMPLE RIDE

Hellions Motorcycle Club

CHELSEA CAMARON

Simple Ride

A Hellions Ride Novella

HELL RAISERS DEMANDING EXTREME CHAOS

USA Today Bestselling Author

Chelsea Camaron

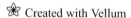 Created with Vellum

BOOMER AND PAM

You took a chance on my books … it brought you to a signing and my table – a meeting I will never forget.

In that short time together, your love shined through. The amazing couple you are, the amazing individuals you are inspires me. I know this book is nothing like your life, but the connection you share made me want to give this couple their own Hellions Ride.

Thank you for being who you are to the core. Thank you for the laughs, the memories, the support, and love. Forever you inspire me.

Love long and love strong that's the Boomer and Pam way.

SIMPLE RIDE

Hellions Ride Book 6

After surviving the heat, the torture, and making it out of the sandbox one mission at a time, I have spent years on the ride, going mile after mile to escape the past. I thought I had left hell behind. Only, it is hard to run from the demons inside you.

It all changed when I found the Hellions brotherhood. My nightmares were chased away with the daylight of my new purpose in the club.

I'm a whore, born from trash; that's what he always told me. Well, sugar, if you can't beat it back, you might as well stop fighting and make the best of it. The Hellions take care of me as long as I take care of their boys, and the arrangement works…

…until he finds me.

Nathan "Boomer" Vaughn—Hellions MC's

newest member, former Army Special Forces, and overall badass—is brought to his knees when he finds out the secrets his favorite barfly has been keeping.

Purple Pussy Pamela should have brought her problems to the club first, but she didn't. Now it's up to Boomer to keep her and her secrets safe.

What happens when two people with a simple understanding complicate things? Can they find their way back to the simple ride?

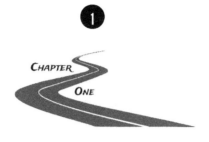

CHAPTER ONE

BOOMER

P*op. Pop. Crack.*
 Boom!

I rise up from my bed, drenched in cold sweat once again. The pillows are tossed to the floor, my blanket twisted into the sheet and hanging off the side, as I blink and gather my thoughts. I am home, safe. My brothers are safe. No one died in my arms tonight. That was my past.

Shaking off the memories, I get up. My room is like everything else in my life—blank. No pictures hang on the walls. My mattress and box spring sit on a basic frame with no headboard, footboard, or adorning features. Blue sheets and a comforter top it until I change them to another color. I have a dresser, no television, no nightstand. Basic, just how I like it.

After quickly fixing my bed, I go to the bathroom and turn on the shower. Shedding my boxer briefs, I then step under the hot water and hang my head in defeat as I let the pressure from the showerhead beat down on my neck.

Will it ever end? Will I ever escape what I did?

Growing up, I had no father to teach me to be a man. I had a single mother who worked three jobs to keep a busted-ass roof over my head and shoes on my always growing feet. As a result, when the recruiter came to my high school and offered me a way out of the small town and a guaranteed paycheck, I couldn't sign up fast enough.

The United States Army.

I never gave it a second thought. I made it through boot camp and was trained to wield a weapon. Expert marksman, sharpshooter, I did it and didn't think beyond completing the next command issued. My MOS—military occupational specialty, or job assignment to civilians—was EOD—Explosive Ordnance Disposal. Get paid to blow shit up? Sign me up.

I worked hard, never allowing myself to really

think through what any of it meant beyond taking care of myself and sending a little back to my mom. I had money in the bank, a job I could be proud of, and more than that, I could take care of the woman who gave up everything for me.

Selection, be one of the elite, a green beret? Again, without hesitation or second thought, sign me up.

It's funny now, as I look back at the young man I was and the man I dreamed to be. I wanted to make my mom proud. I guess I did. She died before I made my first kill. She only knew of her son, the soldier, not the man the Army turned into a weapon. A heart attack took her away from this world, and hopefully, she has found some peace. Maybe in some divine way, it saved her from the heartache of what I would become.

Serve my country with honor, courage, and commitment; protect our freedoms, stand tall, fight hard, and give my all—I did it. Every single thing that was ever asked of me, I did without hesitation or question. Follow orders, be part of the team, and protect our homeland. One of the first things drilled into my head was don't ask questions, react in order.

I was good at my job. It fit me well. My team were my brothers in every way that mattered. Shooter,

Lock, Bowie, Ice, Hammer, Coal, Skid, and Roadie all were as close to me as any family I ever knew, some might even say closer than family. There is a unique bond shared when you trust your life to the skill set of another man.

Only, we failed my last mission. We failed Skid. *I* failed him. The last person he saw was me. The emerald green of his eyes washed away as his blood ran down his face and covered them. The very same blood soaked through my fatigues and still haunts me day and night.

Mission failed, lives lost, and all of us were forever changed.

I took a few years and hit the open road—wild and free, my bike and me. Only, I wasn't free.

Serve my country, I did. Protect our freedoms, I did. However, it came at the cost of my own. I will never be free again. I will never have a moment when his face doesn't haunt me. I will never know what it is to take a breath and not wonder how his young wife is holding up with the son she gave birth to, whom he never had the chance to meet. The little boy has his father's eyes and his mother's smile, and he doesn't get to know the man who made him.

No matter how many miles pass under me, Skid is always with me, reminding me he is gone. It has taken time, but I finally gave up the idea that I could run from the past and have settled into my life here in Catawba, North Carolina.

Shooter and I were always the closest, and I even patched in with the Hellions Motorcycle Club that he is with. This brotherhood is family, too, one I hope to never let down. It took me time to even consider joining, but it has given me a place to belong for the first time since leaving the Army.

Finishing up my shower, I inhale deeply as I dry off. Too much idle time. Unfortunately, I had no skills that could benefit me outside of my military career unless I continued on as a government contractor, a government I swore to protect and uphold, but one that let me down at every turn. No, thank you. My service is done.

Having no one to care for after Mom passed away, I banked my money from every deployment, and I invested it wisely. A medical discharge for a traumatic brain injury gave me a small disability check each month and benefits, so I don't have a regular job. Apparently, getting shot in the head only qualifies me for a percentage.

I lived. Skid died. I get it. Still, I carried his body out with me. That hesitation is what landed the bullet in the back of my skull. I would do it again, all the same. No man left behind. That's not why I carried him, though. He was my brother and had my back, and I promised his wife he would come home. It wasn't the way I intended, but I got him out of the danger before I passed out from my own injuries. Adrenaline is a powerful thing.

Life is lived one moment at a time. In the grand scheme of things, I shouldn't complain. However, it eats away at me inside that a good man with a family was lost, while I lived and have no one.

I pass through life not really living, merely existing. I do what I need to and move on. Occasionally, I perform a demolition job for a few contractors around the country, but mostly, I live alone, ride alone, and outside of the few people I associate with, I like to be alone.

My one bedroom and one bathroom cabin on five acres suits me fine. My closest neighbor is Shooter, who is just as quiet with his family as me. There's less to clean and maintain when it's mostly woods around me. My garage is bigger than my house since I have my truck, my bike, and my mom's old, beat-up Ford Escort that I refuse to get rid of. She worked hard, and that car took me everywhere as a kid.

She haunts me, too. Would she be proud of the man I became? I doubt it. I killed people, a lot of people. Does she understand it was my job? Hell, I don't even understand.

Oh, Momma, if you could see me now...

Money doesn't buy happiness. I don't have to worry about the bills getting paid, but the emptiness inside me never fades.

Pamela

"*You dirty whore, I'll find you. If you ever even dream of leaving me, I'll hunt you down like an animal and gut you. Know your place, bitch.*" *The voice rakes through me, his words sending fear right into my belly.*

He has me against our bedroom wall with his forearm against my stomach, holding me in place as his other hand grips my neck painfully.

"*Your place is with me. For better or worse, you're with me, not her. She's dead to you. I'm your family now, Pamela!*"

"*I wouldn't leave you,*" *I cry out to him.* "*Our family is everything.*"

This is all my fault. I knew I shouldn't have answered her call.

My mother doesn't understand my situation. When she called today, I just knew he would find out, and I would pay the price. I know she wants what's best for me, but she doesn't know. She can't see this side of him. I can't go anywhere. I can't do anything. He will find out. He always does.

"Damn right it is. If you ever leave, you do it without my kids. I'll still kill you, but if you take my kids, I won't make it quick."

Every word is laced in menace, and deep down to my soul, I know he means every threat as a promise. I was young and dumb to tie myself to him, the untamable bad boy I thought I could make love me enough to change.

I was wrong. Dead wrong.

"I'll kill you, Pamela! You hear me? I'll fucking gut you!" He squeezes my neck as he keeps me pinned to the wall. I gasp for air as my lungs burn. "You can't leave me, baby." His voice strains with emotion as the rush finally passes.

His fingers loosen, and then his lips crash down on mine.

I wake up with a jolt. Bringing my fingers to my burning mouth, I touch my lips to prove to myself he isn't here. He hasn't found me. I am safe. My kids are safe. Well, two of them are.

The moment I think of her, tears build behind my eyes, my chest aches, and the emptiness threatens to consume me once again.

Baby Cannon. Oh, my baby girl. My heart bleeds for her.

Although I feel the need to check up on Wesson and Colt, I know Momma would have reached out if anything changed. As long as he doesn't find her, he won't find them. He can find me, but I will die before I give up my sons. They are all I have done right in this world. I couldn't save their sister, but I will be damned if he harms them ever again.

It is too early to go to work, but too close to time for me to get up to go back to sleep.

My new life is not so different from my old one. I clean houses. Doll hired me to clean the office, and I found a new place amongst her family of bikers. I know being a whore to a motorcycle club is far from glamorous. Doll and I have an agreement: as long as I don't mess with the men who have claimed women, then I can hang around the club, and she will make sure I have steady work.

Sure, the agreement began as me cleaning only, but I found the guys had needs. I could make an extra few bucks on my back and also keep myself tucked away. During the day, I go from job to job, cleaning other people's messes while waiting to be found. In the past, I spent my day cleaning *his* messes while waiting for him to find what I missed throughout the day with two tiny toddlers running around and punishing me for it. Now, my nights are spent under the rough hands of a Hellion with their cock pounding away. Before my escape, I spent my nights under the rough feeling of his hands while he pounded away, either with his fists or his dick. I never knew which I would get.

One day at a time, I get by.

I will keep my kids safe. Their future is everything to me, and I will make sure they have a better one than their past.

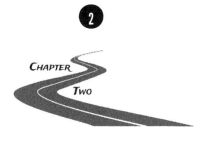

CHAPTER TWO

BOOMER

Something in her eyes calls to me; her soul pulls me to have her close. Underneath the wild woman she portrays is a lost and scared female who is hiding from something. I don't know what, and it certainly isn't my business, but I will do whatever I can to keep her safe when she is with me.

We met under strange circumstances, but call it destiny that I can't walk away from her deep blue eyes, body with curves that call to a man, and a pussy so tight it's like a vacuum sucking my dick deep into her hold.

Pamela is a barfly. She is here to hang around for whatever guy wants to take her home from the club for the night. Most nights in the last year, that man has been me. The rest of the boys see us and have left her to be mine without a problem. This has given us a year to be exclusive without being tied to each other. The truth is that the more time that passes, the more I don't mind the idea of being tied to her.

I have fucked my fair share of women. Pamela, though, she comes alive for me. Either the woman has never had someone give it to her good, or she is one hell of an actress. For me, she gives me purpose beyond just a hole to wet my dick in. I get her off … I get her off like a damn rocket. She takes my cock, and I make her explode.

I am trained in detonation. I wrap my arm around her shoulders, planning to keep her tucked into me all night, smiling to myself when she snuggles closer.

My cock comes to life as I trail my fingers over her shoulder and back up to tickle her neck. She sighs, and I get harder. Then she rolls over on top of me, grinding that purple pussy over my throbbing cock, slickening me with her wetness as she slides over me, rocking her hips.

Her lips come down on mine as I slide my fingers between us and rub her precious nub in a circular motion. Her chestnut brown hair is wild around her face as her eyes, which normally hold such secrets, come alive in ecstasy. *Oh, yeah, Pami, I'm going to make you explode.*

She grinds freely against my hand. Just as her body tightens in anticipation of release, I flip her to her back and roll over her, sliding home as I move us. I rest my weight on my elbows and wrap her legs around my waist. Then, covering her mouth with mine, I let my tongue fiercely tango with hers as she fights to control herself while the sensations keep rolling through her.

My cock slides in and out, in and out. Purposely, I hold the tip steady at her entrance before I slam into her, and she tenses around me as her orgasm crashes through her. I still my cock as her muscles clinch and unclench, milking me. She moans into my mouth before I pull back, sloppily running my tongue over and around her nipples.

She pants beneath me as she tries to gather herself. "Boomer," she whispers breathlessly. Dropping my head, I suck on her nipple hard, causing her to arch up and press me deeper inside her. "Boomer," my name comes off her lips in a needy rasp.

I push back to my knees and move her ankles to

my neck. "Look at me, Pami," I order, and her eyes find mine. So much is hidden in her deep brown orbs.

I rub circles on the inside of her ankles with my thumbs as I slowly move in and out of her pussy. Trailing my right hand down, I let my fingers dance along her skin until I reach her juncture where I rub her pussy lips, feeling the bumps of her poorly done tattoo. She tenses at my touch.

"One day, you will tell me the truth." She closes her eyes at my words. "Look at me, Pami." She again meets my gaze as she pushes my fingers off her folds. "You're safe with me. No matter what our pasts, I'm here in the moment with you. Let go. Be free with me."

I bring both hands to grip her thighs tightly as I increase my pace. As I hit her walls harder and deeper, she tenses while the buildup comes and my balls tighten.

"Boomer," she cries out as her body trembles and shakes beneath me, and I go over the edge, filling her with my very essence and not giving a damn about the possible consequences.

She grabs the back of her legs and drops her ankles off my shoulders, spreading wide as I still fill her with my softening cock. She tries to slide out from me, but I grab her hips and hold her in place, our bodies still connected.

"Don't panic on me now, Pami."

"Panic! Boomer, I feel you hot inside me. You didn't use a condom. Doll is gonna send me packing."

I laugh. "Why would Doll need to know I fucked you raw? What was it you said the first night … 'Boomer, anytime, anywhere, and any way.' Those were your words."

She thrashes her head back and forth as I tighten my grip, keeping her pulled to me. Swiftly, her hand comes up, and then the sting of her slap hits my cheek, the noise filling the room.

Releasing her hips, I bury myself deeper inside her as our bodily fluids mix together around my cock and drip onto the sheets below her. Grabbing her wrists, I pin her arms above her head. Then, leaning down, I breathe on her neck before biting gently.

"Pami, if you wanna play, I'll play. Pain with pleasure works well for me. Doll doesn't have to know I fucked you commando. I'm clean, and I know she makes the girls get checked, so I know you're clean. If you get knocked up … Well, I guess there is another Hellion in the world. What's the problem with that?" I ask, trailing my nose along her collarbone and down to her breasts where I stop to flick each nipple with my tongue.

"No little Hellions." The words come out in a pant, and I know she is getting turned on again.

"Pami, close your eyes," I whisper against her neck. "Picture it, a little girl with your brown hair flowing down her back, deep eyes of whiskey, and my smile. There wouldn't be anyone more beautiful in the world."

She stills, completely freezes. "Stop, Boomer. Stop!" she screams, wrenching her hands free and pushing me off her as she pounds at my chest. "No girls! No kids! Get off me!" She pushes again, this time throwing me off balance and sending me sliding off my own bed. I can't fathom what has her so worked up. "No girls! No kids!" she continues yelling.

"Pami, you know it's more than just fucking between me and you," I say with my ass planted on the floor as she rushes around to gather her clothes.

"No, Boomer! No! No! No!"

A little girl with long, brown hair. My chest physically hurts, and my body aches to be filled with my baby again. Twenty-four weeks gestation … the hospital bed, the pain—it all sits in the forefront of my mind. The contractions wouldn't stop, the rapid succession building and building.

"*Push*," the emergency room nurse who moved me to maternity cried out.

They couldn't stop her from coming. They couldn't stop my body from giving up on her. They said my best hope was the Neonatal team. Only, Cannon Marie Williams was born without the cries of a newborn as she was thrust from the womb. Cannon didn't have the heartbeat of a baby on the path to life.

The doctors and nurses rushed her away to work on her. I listened while, in the corner of the birthing room, they counted the compressions as they fought to bring life back to the blue body of my baby girl. It was a losing battle. She was gone. At his hands, I had lost my name, my body, myself, and more than anything, I had lost my baby girl. Nothing would ever be the same again.

Scurrying around, I throw on clothes without looking at Boomer. We have gotten close over the last year—well, as close as two people can get when you both have secrets, big secrets. Obviously, he is in too deeply with me.

My body trembles as I feel the wetness drip down my leg. Does he have any clue what could have happened if I hadn't had my tubes tied after losing Cannon?

Tears well up in my eyes as I think about his soft words of having a baby with me.

"Pami," he calls out.

"You don't know me," I call out over my shoulder, giving him an ice cold stare.

Walking out of his room, I tug on my clothes and don't look back as I hear him get up. I'm at his front door when I feel him watching me. Turning the knob, I freeze.

"This is how you want it to be?"

I sigh and open the door.

"You makin' your place on your back?" There is sharpness in his tone, finality, it seems. "Pami, it could be on the back of my bike."

I don't look back. I don't stop. One foot in front of the other, I move forward.

"I've always known my place," I whisper as I close the door behind me.

———

One week, six hours, eight minutes, that is how long it has been since I last reached my mother. Anxiety overwhelms me. Wesson and Colt are getting bigger. They are a lot for her to handle, two growing boys. My stomach aches, my heart beats loudly, and my head pounds from thinking of them.

I miss my boys. I miss being a mom to my kids. Without them, I am not me. This self-imposed exile from their lives is slowly killing me.

They are better off without me, though.

They didn't ask to be born. They didn't ask to have Dennis for a father. They didn't ask to be brought into a world of uncontainable fury. They simply didn't ask for anything I gave them. Life with my mom is far from perfect, but it's the only good thing I have ever given them, even if it comes at the sacrifice of me.

Sighing, I clean the bathroom of Crews Transports. Doll makes Tripp and Rex keep it relatively clean, but seriously, a scrub brush and comet are the tools to my day.

Blaine cries out, and I fight to keep my own tears at bay. Doll is blessed to be able bring her baby to work with her. Blaine is a good boy. Tripp, Doll, and little 'BW,' as they call him, are a picture-perfect family. Okay, maybe not your typical picture-perfect, but add leather, ink, and motorcycles, and you can call it the picture-perfect family of badasses.

"Shhhhh, BW, please, baby, please. Momma is losing it here. Daddy will be home in two days. I don't know what to do for you, son," I hear Doll pleading with the toddler.

I come around the corner to see tears streaming down her face. Her blonde hair is tied in a messy knot on her head, and her sweats clearly show she had a rough night.

"You okay?"

When she practically jogs to me and hands BW over, I hold the boy to my hip and rest his head on my shoulder. Then Doll drops her face into her hands.

"I can't do this. He isn't eating right. He has diarrhea. Tripp is gone. He keeps crying. Oh, Pamela, he wails and wails."

I sway back and forth as BW settles against me. "Breathe, Momma, he feels every emotion from you. Get calm, and then we can find the source of his irritation. First, though, he can't feed off you being a mess, making him become a bigger mess." She looks up at me, her red eyes understanding. "If it's a competition of who can cry the longest, baby girl, he's always gonna win, so get your head on straight."

She rolls her shoulders back while I gently pat the diapered bottom of her boy. "*Hush, little baby, don't say a word. Pami's gonna buy you a mocking bird,*" I sing the lullaby and little BW stops crying just enough to take in my soft tone. "That's it, baby boy. *If that mocking bird don't sing, Pami's gonna buy you lots of bling bling.*"

Doll laughs at my change of words, and her son lifts his head to look at her. Once he sees his mom is okay, he settles back against me and closes his eyes as I continue to make up parts of the old song and sway slowly.

"Magic," Doll whispers when she finds that Blaine is soundly sleeping and drooling on my shoulder.

"Teething. I think he's cutting molars. Orajel and Motrin are your new best friends."

She smiles at me in the Doll way that lights up a room. "Right now, Pamela, you are my very best friend."

"Real talk, Doll. You gotta breathe. It's hard when they are little, and it's easy to get overwhelmed, especially when they don't feel well. They can't tell you what's wrong, and not one of us has the ability to read their little minds. But you can't join his pity party because someone has to sort out the world's problems from the view of a two-year-old, and it's not gonna be him."

"You are so wise."

"He is the one person who has heard your heartbeat from the inside, Doll. You are connected in a way no one else can understand. Flesh of your flesh and blood of your blood. What you feel, he feels, so you gotta be rock solid, Momma."

"How many do you have?" Doll asks, watching me carefully. She knows. She can see the mother inside of me. Can she also see the failure I am to my kids?

"That's a problem for another day, Delilah," I answer her honestly, but with her real name so she doesn't press me further.

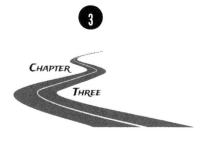

BOOMER

"Pass me the socket wrench set, Axel," I call to Shooter's boy, who is really Rex's son biologically, but somehow in only the way the Hellions can do, Rex and his woman Caroline have found a way to truly co-parent with Shooter and Tessie.

He is an amazing kid. His mom and he brought my best friend out of his own personal darkness and back into the light of life. Mercy was no friend to their ride, but together, they made it through.

"If you don't pull your head outta your ass, I'm gonna sock it to ya," Shooter says from behind me.

"Momma doesn't like those words, Shooter," Axel chimes in, handing me the tool.

Shooter and I both smile.

"What's wrong, Booma?" Axel asks with the childlike innocence that has me frowning.

"Nothing." I turn back to the car in front of me, but a firm hand on my shoulder stops me.

"Come on, man. What's said in the garage blows out the tailpipes, never to be heard from again," Shooter says, making me laugh.

"You're going soft, brother. That was the stupidest thing I have ever heard come out of your mouth, and we both know I have heard some crazy shit."

"Language," Axel chastises. "Momma is gonna be mad at all of us boys if y'all don't clean up your mouths. She even got Lux in on it."

Now that has both Shooter and me laughing. 'Lux' is Caroline, Rex's old lady and his deluxe model woman. She is Fancy Nancy and hell on wheels at the drop of a dime. Ride or die, she's a Hellions ol' lady with fire. They all have that, though. Doll, Sass, Tessie, Lux, Doc Kelly, each one is a badass broad in her own way.

Purple Pussy Pamela is, too; only, she is so caught up in her secrets she holds so close she can't see what's right in front of her.

I am stupid. Completely dumb. Sign me up to wear the dunce cap; that's how badly I fucked up. Men like me don't spout poetic future shit after planting their seed so deep inside a broad it will take days to slide out. No, men like me are supposed to fuck hard, fast, furious, and without thoughts of the future, just raw release. Any other woman would have never given them a second thought. Any other woman never would have gotten the offer.

Pamela did.

I gave her the offer to be on my bike. She knows this world. She knows what that means. Other barflies would have jumped at the opportunity to be claimed in order to have this life and the family it comes with permanently. It isn't an offer to give lightly or to decide on quickly. Pamela did, though.

Pamela walked out. She turned me down.

I have been fucking her for over a year. Then I laid my world at her feet, and she walked away. She didn't look back. She hasn't called.

"It's nothing, man," I try to brush him off.

"Then stop looking at your phone and the door like you've gotta take off in an instant."

I take pause to focus on my latest behaviors. He is right; I have been watching my phone and door like a fucking lovesick teenager.

This stops now!

No broad needs to have this kind of power over a man. Even more so, I don't really know her other than she sucks my cock like it's her job. Oh, wait, I guess it is. She keeps the club happy, and the club keeps her in our fold. I guess she showed me my place.

I run my hand over my beard in frustration. "My mind is all over the place."

"Get your head on straight."

"Wanna blow stuff up, Booma?" Axel pipes in, going to the toolbox for Shooter.

I laugh. "Why would you ask that?"

"My dad always tells Lux he needs to blow a load. Your name is Booma 'cause you make things go boom, I reckon … so you wanna find some stuff to blow up?"

"Always, little man, always. We better get this car finished first, though."

"Sounds good to me. Shooter has the good fire-works hidden in the shed." He smiles brightly.

"Hey, that was a secret," Shooter jokes.

"Bro code. Booma needs bro time, and what better way than lighting stuff on fire and watching it go up? It's on a need to know basis"—Axel makes a serious face at Shooter—"and he really needed to know. We've got his back, Shooter; you tell me that all the time. Family and shi—stuff. Stuff, right? Booma is family. He gets bro code."

Shooter ruffles his hair. "Totally."

After fixing the car and making some stuff go boom, I leave Shooter and Axel to head to the bar. I am playing with fire, and one of us is going to get burned for sure.

The place is slow for the usual Saturday night crowd at Ruthless. Then again, since Tessie's attack, only Hellions hang around here, keeping it light and tight.

Kerri comes around the corner, looking every bit the sex kitten she is in a super short mini skirt that lets her ass cheeks hang out.

"Hey, Boomer," she purrs as she slides on the bar stool next to me, her breasts filling out her shirt to maximum capacity.

I lift my beer to her and tip it back without speaking. Throwing my hand up, I get Corinne's attention for another long neck. She makes a face before popping the top and slamming the glass bottle down in front of me.

"Watch yourself," I warn Corinne. "Know your place." I'm not about to take any disrespect from a damn barfly.

Out of the corner of my eye, I see Pamela come

around from the back where the bathrooms are. She glares at me and then Kerri, and I smile as I take another pull of the beer. Yeah, misery loves company, and she had her chance.

Tracking her movements in my peripheral vision, I am surprised when she drops to her knees beside my barstool. When I turn to her, my eyes burn with desire, and my mind races with thoughts of what she could be hiding behind that cold stare. Her hands slide up the inside of my thighs as her gaze remains locked on mine.

"If it's a showdown you want, baby, it's a showdown you're gonna get." I smirk, taking a long drink and watching the condensation drop from my bottle into the open cleavage of her chest. Oh, if only to be that small drop of water sliding down the peaks and into the valley of sweetness.

My cock throbs in my jeans as it pulses against the zipper. Her fingers come up to my button when I reach down with my free hand and stop her.

"What are you doing, Pami?" I ask honestly, wondering what she really thinks right now.

"I know my place." She smirks at me, each word laced in menace.

"On your knees, on your back, doesn't really

matter to me. You're not my business anymore." I push her hands off me, forcing her to lean back so as not lose her balance, giving me enough room to stand.

"Boomer," she calls out as I walk to the back room where the pool tables are.

I don't look back as I tell her, "That ship has sailed, woman. That ship has fuckin' sailed."

Pamela

Go to work, come home, and check in with the club every few days. Survive, get by, and keep my bastard husband away from my kids. Sitting in my chair in my shithole trailer, I rub my empty belly absently.

Ghost flutters.

I feel them. I feel her. Even though she is gone, I feel her inside me. The pull is so deep I could drown in the misery.

My only responsibility and priority is to my children, and I failed her. In my head, I can hear the rapid beating of her tiny heart, the heart I longed to hear at every doctor's appointment. The swishing and steady *thump, thump, thump* were heaven to my ears. In one night, in the flash of one mistake, she was gone.

I didn't deserve her. I don't deserve Wesson and Colt. God took her to keep her for his own, for I am weak and undeserving of such a precious life. Wesson and Colt were my gifts. They were my opportunity to see the light and get away.

I didn't listen to my gut. I didn't take the many opportunities I was given to leave. I failed to walk through every door that was opened to me. As a little girl, Momma took me to Sunday school where we sang songs and learned Bible verses. The trainings of a child, the motto, the chant—if he leads you to it, he will get you through it.

I balked.

Every time I could leave and should have, I froze. From the moment I knew she existed, I knew in my heart, deep into my very soul, it was going to be the end this time.

"Fucking kids!" Dennis roars. "Lazy-ass white woman can't pick up one fucking thing." He stomps into our tiny living room and throws a mangled tricycle at my boys.

I rush in front of them, putting myself between them and the monster who helped conceive them. Not my babies. No way, no how. Do whatever the hell you want to me, but not my boys. No one will touch my boys until I'm cold and dead. .

He marches over to me, standing toe to toe. I will not back down, though. He cannot punish my boys. Not today, not ever, but especially not today. The tricycle was outside because I was trying to get them to wear out and take a good nap. I have had the flu for the last week and my period came this morning, so I was tired. After outside play, the three of us lay down. I didn't plan to sleep this long, but having two boys under two is hard. I was going to bring them out before dinner and then clean up.

Dinner.

He is really going to flip when he finds out dinner isn't ready.

I wave my hand behind my back, trying to shoo the boys away. They don't move. He does.

His breath comes down hot on my neck. "Lazy bitch," he mutters as he raises his hand high in the air. The smack comes down, and I bite my lip so hard I bleed, trying not to cry out from the pain. The copper taste does nothing except send my adrenaline into overdrive. Then the punch to my stomach comes, hunching me over, and I bend farther to watch my little ones hurry away.

Hide, little ones, *I think to myself.*

In my distraction, I don't prepare for the knee that comes to my face. I fall backward onto my ass as he climbs over me. My sweatpants are yanked down harshly as he straddles me, slapping my face from side to side and laughing with each roll of my neck.

He's the dog, and I'm his toy.

I close my eyes as I feel him stand and undo his pants. Then he straddles me again, pushing my shirt up and moving my bra to rest on top of my large breasts, painfully constricting my chest. His cock is hard, sliding over my belly while he pinches my tender nipples painfully. I want to vomit.

"Love that cock, baby," he groans as he squishes my breasts together and slides between them. "Titty fuck me good. Fuck my anger away. That's right, my Pamela, fuck it all away."

He scoots down and parts my legs, no doubt seeing my pants and bloody pad. He now knows this is not an ideal time, but does he care? No. He slams into me and pounds away, and my stomach lurches as my insides ache while he slaps my stomach to match each thrust.

"Gush for me, Pamela, gush," he cries out as I feel wetness leak out of me. All I can think of is the mess on my carpet as he finally fills me with his release.

He slides out and his face pales. "Sick, bitch. Clean this up." He stands to pull his pants up, and I see his blood-covered cock. I want to vomit, but more so, I wish it was his own blood covering his limp dick and not mine.

Dennis goes to shower and change, leaving me aching and a mess, emotionally and physically.

Slowly, I manage to make dinner while he showers —tatortot casserole is quick and easy. I feel my period getting heavier with every move I make. Somehow, I get through the night without disturbing him as I bleed through multiple times.

Once he leaves for work, I make the emergency call to my mom to watch the boys. Then I drive two counties over to the free clinic where I know they won't push me about the bruises covering my face. I check in, and the nurse quickly offers me a rape kit that I laugh off.

"No, I've never bled this heavily, even after having my kids, so I just want to make sure everything is okay."

She smiles a polite smile that screams she doesn't believe me. After I pee in a cup, they take blood, and then I climb on the table, naked from the waist down, holding a pad to myself because I don't want to bleed on the table while I wait for the doctor.

She is a gray-haired lady who is obviously ready to retire. She looks at my chart, looks at me, and leaves the room. Well, no one promises good bedside service at a free clinic.

She wheels in the ultrasound machine and pushes me back on the table. She wraps the wand with a condom while the nurse settles my feet into the stirrups, and she removes the pad. The wand goes in, and my body clinches automatically.

The rhythmic swish lulls me as I hear the steady thump of a strong heartbeat. Immediately, I cry. I know those sounds. That is the sound of my baby.

My baby girl. She made it through that night. I was nine weeks along, and the doctor felt she'd possibly had a twin that I lost, causing the bleeding. She couldn't promise I wouldn't lose this one, so I needed to take it easy and return in two days for blood work.

Two days turned into fifteen more weeks of one hard pregnancy, a pregnancy that wouldn't make it full-term and would kill a part of me every single day after its loss. I should have left then. I didn't, and my baby girl paid the price. My boys now do, too, living as someone they aren't with my mother. They can't know me.

When my phone rings, I look at the screen as dread fills me.

Unknown number.

"Hello?" I answer.

"Hello, Pamela." Chills run down my spine at his voice. "I'm coming for you."

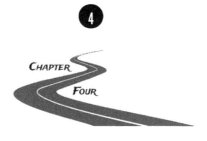

4

BOOMER

I am a dick. I wasn't raised to be a dick, but I sure have become one.

What's the best way to get over pussy? Get balls deep in another one. Pamela had me for the last year. That ship has sailed.

I slap Keri's ass. "Time to go," I say, getting up and going to the motel bathroom without looking back. Then I freshen up, hoping she's gone before I get out.

No such luck.

"Time to go," I say again.

She is dressed and sitting on the edge of the bed. Her hair is wild, like we are back in the eighties, and her makeup is smeared. I know she got it good from me last night, so why hang around?

"Secrets, Boomer."

"What about them, Keri?" I snap.

"We all got 'em."

"Time to go," I repeat firmly.

"I'm not talking about yours, Boomer; I know better. I'm talkin' about Purple Pussy Pamela. You and her, I see it. Last night, you called out her name. I was sucking you off since my pussy couldn't get the job done. I'm fucking and sucking, only for it to be her on your mind."

"Watch yourself, Keri."

"Secrets, Boomer, just think about it. She's got 'em; you've got 'em; and not that anyone cares, I've got 'em, too. She cares about you, but the girl's got secrets."

"Last I checked, you're a barfly, Keri, not a love doctor."

"Love has nothing to do with it. I'm a woman who sees a woman who could use a friend. You're the only one she's let close."

"What is this, the sisterhood now? You should shut the fuck up."

"Get your head outta your ass, Boomer. You're better than that. All the Hellions, badass as you are, have got a heart. That woman needs a friend. Be that friend, Boomer."

Without another word, she leaves while my anger boils.

Who the fuck does she think she is? I'm a mother fucking Hellion, and she wants to tell me to get my head outta my ass? No more fucking that one.

I rub my beard. She sure wasn't telling me to get my head from between her legs. Even if I was picturing a purple pussy with polka dots while I ate her hard, she still got hers.

I grumble as I gather my wallet, phone, and helmet. Then I set the no-tell motel room key on the bed and leave.

Getting on my bike, I hit the open road and don't look back.

The mountains take my focus. My mind can't drift. The gravel is solid beneath me, the wind blowing against my face, and the miles breeze by.

I haven't been this twisted since I came home and faced Melonie.

She pounds on my chest, crying, sobbing, and her belly shaking with the baby inside who doesn't know what he lost.

"He promised to love, honor, and protect, Boomer." She pounds against my chest. "How can he protect me from the grave? How can he honor me when he's no longer with me? He promised forever, Boomer," she screams at me, hitting again with each word. "He promised to love me forever."

"He did, he does, he will," I reply as I take each hit from the grieving widow in my arms.

She stills, looking at me with swollen eyes, the tears falling down her face. "You ever been in love, Boomer?"

"No, I can't say that I have," I reply honestly.

"It's all-consuming. I can't breathe without him."

I can't breathe. The entire world stops in this moment. My brother in arms is gone, and his pregnant wife is hurting. She is going to live the ultimate sacrifice. I thought leaving on each mission, fighting, and killing were the sacrifices I made for my country. I thought my duty, my life on the line, was the greatest risk and the greatest pain to bear.

I was wrong.

I was wrong. The greatest pain is to survive; the greatest sacrifice is to those who are left behind. Melonie made the greatest sacrifice to our country, my country, in losing the man she loved, the man she had built a life with and trusted with her future. She gave it up in the name of freedom.

Where I am weak, she is strong. It hasn't been easy, but she has gotten by for herself and for Taylor, their son.

I ride on. I press forward. The sounds around me fade to the steady tick of the engine beneath me. I could do this forever.

I was made for solitary life.

Then, as if I was being slapped in the face, I remember the sensation of her wrapped around me. I remember the pull of Pami's fingers on my stomach and the squeeze of her thighs around me. Her presence soothes me.

Why?

She's no different to me than Keri: a place to dip my stick every so often; release given and taken, no strings. So why do I want Pami on my bike? Why, in the middle of my darkest of thoughts, does my mind go back to her? Why can she pull me out of the sadness and make me want nothing more than to turn around and go back?

How, in all this time of riding free, do I suddenly find someone who can call me back home yet doesn't want me there?

Secrets.

We all have them. Keri is right about that.

What would my purple-pussy lover think if she knew it would have been better to have been me that died, not Skid? What would everyone think if they knew that, in my mind, I beg to go back and take his place? I want nothing more than to trade my life for his. I have no woman, no love, no kid, no family … He had it all, lost it all, and here I am, running away again.

One of the elite, my ass.

I am nothing more than a pawn in Uncle's Sam's game against the world, now reduced to a bitter former soldier, the warrior inside me dead.

My stomach burns. My chest aches. There is nothing left to fight for.

Pamela

Don't panic. Don't panic. He will not win, I remind myself over and over to stay calm.

If he knew where I was, I would certainly be dead. If he knew where the boys were, I would be dead. I can't mess this up by becoming careless now.

Absently, I rub my belly, the place where each of

my children began. Day by day, they grew inside of me. My body provided them safety, nutrition, and love from the very beginning. I lost my precious baby girl, but I won't lose my boys.

He hasn't found them, I tell myself over and over. *Think, Pami, think. How did he find me?*

Absently, I straighten up my trailer, refusing to peek out of the windows. If he's watching, I won't give him the satisfaction of rattling me. Maybe he only has my phone number … Hopefully, he hasn't found me yet.

Time to plan.

Today, I have to clean Doll's house. Then I will give her my one-week notice. I can't make any sudden moves if he has found me.

Going to the kitchen, I take out the cereal box—Lucky Charms, their favorite. I smile, thinking of my boys and the many times they have probably had this since I have been gone. My wish is for the end of the rainbow.

I pull out the money I have been saving and count it out. Although three thousand dollars won't get me far, it will get me to another state and set up until I can find a job waitressing or something.

I hate to leave North Carolina, but if he's found me, being in the same state as my boys is too close. If he can find me in Catawba, he can find them on the coast. Maybe my mistake was moving them and me to small towns. Maybe the city would hide us better. I will keep that in mind for my next location. Then, when it's safe, maybe Momma should go to Raleigh or Charlotte. I now know I won't keep us in the same state again, so wherever she goes, it will be far from wherever I am. Of course, that is going to take money, too.

Tears fill my eyes. I send her all I can. The Hellions pay well, but what will happen at the next place? I may not make enough.

I got too comfortable. I stayed too long. That's how he found me. Now I have to uproot my boys again because of my mistakes.

Will they ever get to live their lives out of the shadow of the past? Will they ever get to be free from the poor decisions I have made over and over again?

My heart hurts, and the tears freely fall as I can't hold them back. Focus, I have to focus. Just like when I made the move to leave, I must be careful and every step must be thought out. I can do this. I can start over and keep my boys away from him.

I make it to Tripp and Doll's house on time physically. Mentally, I am a million miles away from the Catawba Hellions president's house.

I am dusting the entertainment center when, for what seems like the millionth time today, I drop something. Specifically this time, I drop Tripp and Doll's wedding picture.

I pick up the shattered frame as tears fill my eyes again. The love and happiness between them is seen in the photo. Their children will get to look at this and know they came from real love. My boys won't get to see pictures like that.

I was knocked up with Colton, and my ex said let's go to the courthouse so I could be on his work insurance. There are no pictures, and in my memories —if I block out what happened after that day—it was a happy occasion. Unfortunately, it is one of very, very few good memories.

I thought he would give me the world. After all, there are few men out there who would marry a chick they knocked up after only going out three times. There are few men out there who would so easily step up and take care of their responsibilities.

On the flip side of the same coin, I would like to believe there are few men out there who wish to dominate, control, and manipulate someone they claim to love. Deep in my soul, I would like to believe there are few men out there who relish in the power of bringing pain upon someone they love.

Deep in my heart, I would like to believe in the power of real love. I would like to believe unconditional love does exist.

I don't want to become a man hater. I don't want to become a jaded, bitter woman. I simply want to be me. I want to be loved for my talents as well as my shortcomings. I want to be accepted for my beauty and my scars. I want to be me. I want to be loved from the inside out. I want to heal from the past and look forward to the future. I want someone who can take on my baggage and carry the load with me. I want to believe this can still be possible for me and for my sons.

I have to get my emotions under control.

I sweep up the fragments on the floor and carefully remove the picture. I clean the glass out of the frame and save the shell in case this one means something to Doll. I will pay for a new frame or have the glass replaced in this one, whichever she chooses.

I sigh and mumble to myself, "Get it together, Pami. Every penny counts."

I am just about done cleaning when Doll comes in from grocery shopping. I help her unpack her belongings before getting ready to leave.

"I accidentally dropped the picture and it broke. I'm sorry. I'll pay for a new frame or the glass if you want to use the same frame," I go ahead and let her know as I hand her the photo and the frame.

She looks at it and smiles. "Best day of my life other than having BW."

I open the envelope of cash she had left to pay me today when she reaches out and touches my hand.

"No worries. I can get a new frame." She pauses and takes me in. "Why are you shaking?"

Always perceptive, the tiny blonde is. I should have known she would see through me.

"I need to give my notice." My voice cracks on the final word.

"Oh, hell no. Triple P, that ain't happening. Do you know how hard it is to find someone I can trust in my house when I'm not home? No, not accepted. If you need more money, consider it done. If you need a better place to stay, Tripp will make that happen. I'm not looking for a new cleaner. I need someone I can trust at the business and at home. You're it, Pami, and I'm not letting you go."

Pride fills me and my heart swells. No one has ever wanted to keep me around except my own mom. I finally found a place I belong, and I have to give it up. I have to for my boys.

"It's not the money, Doll."

"Okay, so I told you when you applied we could

get you a nicer place to stay if you wanted. Tripp can get it done in a matter of days. The boys can move your stuff."

"No," I stop her from planning. "I don't mind my place. I told you before I don't need anything fancy. I am fine in my trailer."

"Then what?" she asks, genuinely concerned. "Is your mom sick? We can move her here." She states it so simply.

Oh, what a joy it would be to have my mom and boys with the Hellions where I know he couldn't get to them. I can't do that, though. I can't burden the club with my problems.

"I didn't plan to stay here this long, Doll. I'm a free spirit, you know. It's time to move on."

"I don't believe you," she states. That's Doll, never one to hold back punches.

"I have someone who means something to me. I have to handle it," I say, tiptoeing around the truth.

"Aw, Pami, why didn't you tell me you're in love?" she adds excitedly.

"It's not exactly like that. You just gotta know when to take a chance."

"I understand taking chances. Oh, Pami, we are gonna miss you, but I understand."

"I'll finish out the next week, and if you want me

to train Corinne, Keri, or someone else, I'd be glad to. I need to leave by next Saturday, though."

"Thanks for the heads up, and this gives us time to plan a going away party." She claps her hands happily.

Oh, Doll, this is far from a happy occasion.

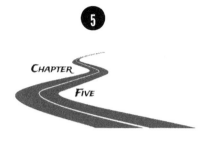

BOOMER

After two days away, my mind isn't any clearer than it was before.

My phone rings with an unknown number. It could be a potential client, so without thinking, I answer.

"How's that pussy been treating you?"

"Excuse me? Who the fuck is this?" I ask.

"I marked her; she's mine."

"What the fuck are you talking about?"

"You shouldn't fuck another man's wife. That

pussy has my mark. You're gonna pay and so is she. Once I find my sons, you're both dead."

Silence.

I look at my phone screen, seeing the call ended. My mind runs wild. Keri? Does Keri have a husband? And sons? Was that her reference to secrets?

Anger boils in my veins. Some crazy-ass mother-fucker just threatened my life over a piece of pussy. I don't know him or his fucking wife.

Sure, I fuck around, but I have no ties to anyone. I asked Pami, and she declined, so I have no ol' lady to respect. The pussy I fuck is consensual, and it damn sure isn't married.

What secrets does Keri have? What shit storm is she bringing to the club?

The barflies are given a background check, but they don't get any club business, so it's not the most thorough. It might be time we reevaluate this policy on the hang-around whores. Someone has secrets, and secrets in a motorcycle club cost lives. No life of a brother is worth a piece of pussy.

Looking at the phone, I make the call. The Hellions need to know there is something going on, even if it turns out to be nothing.

"Shooter," I bark into the phone.

"Brother," he answers calmly. That is Shooter: always collected.

"Ride out."

"Where to?"

That simple response is what defines the Hellions. No questioning why, just take your brother's back whenever he calls. Shooter would have my back club or no club, but he will make sure Tripp, Rex, and the rest of the crew are there to back me up if needed.

"I'm a day and half away. Round up Keri. Fuck, find out about all the bitches at Ruthless. Every barfly who is affiliated needs to be checked." I try to think rationally. It may not be her husband calling me.

"Consider it done. Where do you want Keri when you return?"

"Somewhere no one can find her before I get there."

"You good, man?"

"Just need some questions answered, not just for me, but for the whole fucking club."

Shooter sighs. "If shit is gonna rain down on the club, I gotta know now, Boomer."

Honesty is part of loyalty. "I don't know. I got a call. Someone has a husband, one who apparently has a wife and sons he wants back."

"Fuck!" Shooter loses his cool demeanor.

He has a son—stepson, but Axel is as much his flesh and blood as Tessie and Rex. If someone took Tessie and Axel from him, he would go crazy. If someone kept them hidden, he would go after whoever stood in his way.

"Day and half tops," I remind.

"Consider it handled." Shooter clicks off.

Without another thought, I set off for home. Fuck with me, fine. Bring shit to my brothers' doorsteps, and we have a problem. Barfly or not, the Hellions won't tolerate problems from an outsider. Whoever her ex is, he just made his last threat.

The motherfucker is going to die, and if I have it my way, it will be at my hands for that phone call.

———

The old hunting cabin is one room, no decorations. We keep it for the times we need to hide someone or, in this case, question someone. A fireplace lines one wall with a couch to the side of it. There is a toilet that has a shower curtain hanging for privacy. It's a shithole, but serves its purpose well. Sitting off the beaten path, no one can find it unless they are looking.

Shooter and Rex are on the porch talking when I pull up. Shooter's short hair is a contrast to the man bun Rex is sporting. Two completely opposite men, but after a long road between them, they have a bond that is thicker than blood.

"Boomer, how goes it, brother?" Rex greets.

"Helluva ride," I reply, stepping onto the porch. "She in there?"

"Yeah, we checked her out, too. She has an ex-husband. Cop," Rex answers my next question before I can ask.

"Kids?" I wonder if she is the one now.

"Can't have them," Shooter answers.

"Let's go have a chat with the wife of a boy in blue," I say, irritated that she has covered her past that well.

"Ex," Shooter corrects.

"Last pussy I fucked sits in there, the same pussy that wanted to bring up secrets the morning after. We've all got secrets, she said. Two days later, I have some stranger calling me about fucking his wife and wanting his sons. The cop was a secret, so what else is she hiding?"

"True, but I don't think she's the one," Rex says.

We enter and see Keri sitting on the couch,

looking tired. Her eyes are swollen from crying, her makeup smeared, and her hair is a complete mess.

"Boomer?" She looks up at me.

My eyes go cold. I feel the betrayal. She knows more than she has let on.

"Secrets, Keri."

She blows out a breath. Rex leans against the wall casually, crossing his legs at the ankles, while Shooter stands at the door. I stand in front of her, scowling down at her.

"What did you mean the other day about secrets?"

"We all have them," she whispers, her lip quivering.

Fatigue from my ride and the anger that someone threatened me have me at my breaking point. Reaching down, I wrap my hand around her throat, squeezing just enough to get her attention and hold her still.

She reaches up and holds my wrists, trying to relieve the pressure.

"Enough with the word games. What the fuck are you talkin' about?"

Her eyes grow wide. "Secrets," she chokes out in a whisper.

I push her back against the couch and straddle her. Releasing her neck, I grab her hands and hold them over her head. I put my nose to hers, my beard hitting her chin with every word I speak.

"What fuckin' secrets?"

Tears fill her eyes again. "Boomer, please."

"I'm an asshole, so pleading won't help you. I could give a shit what the hell happens to you. You keep talking about secrets, but you don't share them, and now I've got some man threatening me over pussy and secrets. It's time to start talking, Keri. We know you've got a cop husband."

She tenses under me at the mention of him. Ah, good to know he still has some effect on her.

She blinks slowly as if fighting some emotion. "Ex-husband and ex-cop."

"Where is he now? Where are his sons?"

Panic fills her eyes. "Sons?" she asks, and that's when I realize it isn't her. "Henley and I didn't have kids. He's remarried with a little girl. I'm not the one with the secrets you should be digging into."

I jerk off of her harshly.

If it isn't her, then who is it? A thought hits me. It can't be. No way would she have that kind of secret.

At the same time, I begin to think it, Keri moves to stand. Her soft hand reaches out, and she rubs the side of my beard gently.

"You should be keeping Pamela close right now.

You should be asking her the questions you're asking me. I'm sorry, Boomer."

Anger, fury, and rage—I see red as I am consumed in madness. I pull her hand off my face, jerking her up as I do, and put back her to the wall as Rex moves out of the way.

"She's not here; you are. What do you know?"

Fear fills her eyes again. She should be afraid. She has kept secrets from the club, secrets that could have Pamela in danger.

"I don't know much. A man found me outside of Ruthless the night before we hooked up last. He tried to pay for sex. When I said no, that we are for the club, he asked about special pussy, marked pussy, where he could find marked pussy."

The truth hits me like a wrecking ball. Marked pussy. Pamela's tattoo covers scars; I have felt them.

Keri keeps talking while my mind spins.

"I said, if he's looking for hookers, he needs to go to the city, not out here. He said he was exactly where he needed to be; he just needed a release before he found his woman again. He rambled about a wife named Pamela and two sons. He was half-crazy."

"Half-crazy and you didn't think to tell a brother?" I roar.

"I told you people had secrets. You've got a thing

for Purple Pussy Pamela, so I figured you would seek her out and sort this."

Fucking Pamela... What the hell kind of baggage does she have?

Pamela

Ruthless is slow, and I am thankful for that.

Corinne is behind the bar. I look at her, the closest thing I have to a real friend, and hate myself. I should have told her. I should have told someone.

"Hey girl, what's up?" she greets as I slide onto a barstool.

"Can I borrow your phone to make a call? Mine is dead," I ask, knowing this is my only hope. If Dennis is watching me, I can't use my phone to check in. I have a burner phone, but I don't want him to get suspicious.

"Sure. It's in my purse in the office." She smiles then moves to wipe down the bar.

I make my way to the back, shutting the office door behind me. He can't see in here. I haven't seen anyone around that resembles my ex, but I don't want to take any chances.

Not being able to call and verify he hasn't gotten to the boys has killed me, but I have to be smart. I have to stay a step ahead. Maybe all he has is my phone number.

A girl can dream, right?

I get Corinne's purse out of the bottom desk drawer and make the call to the prepaid phone I have set up for my mom.

"Hello?" she answers cautiously.

"Hey, Ma." I swallow back tears from hearing her voice.

"Pami." She doesn't hide the delight and relief in her tone.

"He called."

I hear her gasp into the phone. "We have to go." She begins to jump into action.

"No, you stay put. I think you're safe. But I can't be in contact for a while, and I can't send money until I get reestablished somewhere."

"Pami, please go to the police. Get help."

"I can't, Ma. He would still get visitation, and I don't want a monster like him around my boys. I know he will find a way to kill me, anyway, police or no police. Just keep the boys safe and give them my love."

"I'll die before anyone gets to them."

"I know, Ma. That's why they're with you." Tears fall down my face. "I love you."

"I love you, precious."

"I've gotta go," I whisper, not wanting to end the call.

"I know. Be safe, my daughter."

The line goes dead, killing another piece of my heart.

I miss my boys. I miss my mom. However, I can't be with them and keep them away from him. I would die to give them freedom.

I walk out of the office and bump right into someone. Backing away, I look up into the dark brown eyes of a man on a mission.

Boomer.

Dammit, this is not helping things.

I inhale deeply, taking in the masculine scent of leather and Boomer. I stop myself from reaching out to touch him.

He wants to give me more. He wants to give me himself. Nathan 'Boomer' Vaughn thinks he's a bad man, but he is really everything a woman could want.

Strong, loyal, honest, caring, and fierce are just a few characteristics that make up the man behind the cut.

My body and mind come alive whenever he is near. Today is no different. ·

"Where you off to in such a hurry?" he asks as his eyes bore into mine, seeking something.

"I have work to do," I stammer, trying to wipe the tears from my eyes.

"Work, huh?" He is pissed, but right now, I can't allow myself to care.

"Boomer, I don't have time for this right now. I'm late to clean a business. I can't afford to lose this client," I lie.

"I'll pay double their rate for an hour," he says calmly, and I see red.

Reaching back, I swing, not thinking of the consequences, and slap him across the face.

"I'm no one's hooker. Fuck you, Boomer! Fuck. You!" I storm off as he holds his hand to his face in shock by my reaction.

I have to get out of here. Boomer was the only one I thought saw me as more than pussy. He wanted something real not so long ago. Now I'm just ass he's willing to pay for. Well, fuck that and fuck him. I have enough on my plate.

Why didn't I just leave when I got the call? Why

did I bother to give Doll notice? It's not like I'm going to need references. I need nothing to tie me to North Carolina.

He found my number; he may have found me. That means finding my sons will be next.

I cannot and will not let that happen. With my dying breath, he will not get my boys.

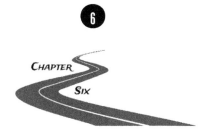

CHAPTER SIX

6

BOOMER

What the hell is she running from? During all this time we have been together—not just fucking, but pillow talk and what I would consider a developing relationship—how could she not know I would help her? How can she think for one second the club wouldn't back her?

It hits me—she's not claimed.

I offered her that spot. I have been with my fair share of women, but none have been like a balm to my wounded soul like Pamela. Now something is going on, and she won't be honest with me.

Why?

A husband? Sons? Is Pamela married with kids? She doesn't strike me as the type to leave her kids behind. She has a soft side, a nurturing side that I don't think would allow her to be separated from her kids.

My mind goes crazy with questions while my cheek stings from her slap.

Did she really think I was offering to pay her for sex? Is her idea of the man I am that distorted?

Asshole, most definitely, but scum who pays for sex, I am not.

I would never think of her like that. The club doesn't pay barflies for sexual services. No woman has to do anything she doesn't want to. They are given a place to hang out, plenty of booze to drink. We help them with jobs, help them have a place to stay, and when they want to, they are around to fuck whichever available Hellion they choose. The only rule is don't mess with the Hellions who have ol' ladies. The barflies stay clean, and we help them out. They can leave at any time.

I clutch my chest. She's going to leave. I feel it. Dammit, I am fucking this up at every turn.

"Boomer," Shooter calls out, and I realize I am

still standing in the same spot, dumbfounded. As I turn to him, he studies me. "You feel it?"

I raise an eyebrow at him in question.

"The pull? The drive? The need? The fire? She yours?" His last question hits me square in the gut.

"Abso-fuckin-lutely." I feel every bit of it. For the first time since my momma died, I feel.

Absently, I rub my chest. I fucking feel it. Pamela better look out because I'm coming for her, and I expect answers.

He smiles. "Then we need to follow your woman, not stand here."

I've spent too many years riding around aimlessly. I've spent too much time trying to outrun the past instead of looking toward the future. Pamela is the only person in all this time to give me a reason to think about anything good.

The things I have seen, the things I have done, they don't hold me back when she's around. I get tunnel vision. I get lost in her. She has this softness to her, this look in her eyes that tells of a woman who has been through hell and fought her way out. I know that look. I see it in the mirror every damn day. Only, I can't find my way out without her.

Kids? Does she really have sons?

"Need intel before we chase her. She's running

scared. Just need to figure out if it's from me or someone else."

"I'll make the call," Shooter says, reaching for his phone.

Going to the bar, I slide in front of Corinne, and she gives me a half smile.

I fucked her a few times before Pamela. She's a hellcat in bed. She goes wild, but she gets lost somewhere in her mind, and it becomes as much a release for her as me. The connection just doesn't happen.

She has secrets, too. They all do. Keri was right about that. Only, their secrets don't bother me. Pamela's do.

Could she have a husband? In all this time we have shared together, I know she is the kind of woman you bring home to your mom. She knows how to be a lady on your arm and the mistress in your sheets. I have a hard time believing my Purple Pussy Pamela would make a lifelong commitment and not stand by it.

Marked pussy... The words come back to my mind.

I have spent countless hours with my face between those thighs, my lips on those lips, and my tongue diving deep into her core. Each of those orange polka dots is over raised flesh—marked flesh.

Marked pussy.

Bile builds up in my throat, but I swallow it down. He marked her lips. Did he do the tattoo? Or is that her way of hiding him?

Although Corinne sets a beer in front of me, I can't bring myself to touch it.

"What did she want?" I ask, trying to stop my stomach from churning.

"She needed to use my phone."

"I need your phone then and the last call you made."

She shakes her head yet moves for me to know she is giving in. I follow her back to the office where she hands me the device. It is still mildly wet, probably from the tears Pamela was fighting to push back.

Who did she call? Why was she crying?

I go through the call log … Last call, Devlin. I look at the time. Three hours ago.

Not her call.

In frustration, I throw the phone. It hits the back wall, and Corinne runs after it. The screen is cracked, and she looks ready to kill.

Well, guess what? So am I!

I open my wallet and toss out five hundred dollars. "If that's not enough, I'll get you more later. I've gotta find your friend."

I don't wait for her to reply. I don't give a shit. Pamela was smart to delete the call. But why was it necessary?

What makes a woman hide so much? What makes a woman who is as loyal, as I have learned she is, leave a husband?

Did she dupe me? Was it all a façade, or is she in trouble?

The man on the phone had no problems threatening me. He knows nothing of the trained killing machine I am, yet he had the balls to threaten me. She has marks on her pussy lips from him, no doubt about it.

Rage consumes me. I see red.

He hurt her. He hurt her in the most damaging ways imaginable. And in all this time, she has held onto her secrets, her pain. She held it in. She has given me an outlet. Time and again, she has been there for me to get lost in or simply to be with. However, she has kept her own struggles to herself. She has carried her own burdens without anyone to share the load.

Well, baby, she better hold on tight because she's not alone anymore. I'm going to find the fucker that hurt her, and I'm going to make him pay.

Pamela

M istakes happen when people get distracted, and I am officially distracted as I make my way to my trailer. My heart hurts that Boomer would think he could pay me for my time. I thought Boomer and I had something semi-real.

Who am I kidding? He knows nothing about the real me. If Boomer knew my past, he would have never touched me in the first place. To think he could pay me cuts deeply, though.

I'm not a hooker. A whore, obviously, but it happened for a reason. I needed a place where I felt safe. The Hellions gave me that until he found me. It's been a good run, but now it's time to move on.

Without thinking, I step inside, my mind on Boomer. It needed to be on survival, because I make it two steps inside before I am grabbed from behind, his breath hot on my neck.

"Hello, dear," he snarls as he tightens his forearm around my throat.

I pull at him, but he is bigger, and I have never stood a chance against him.

"I think it's time we have a little chat. First,

though, we should get reacquainted. It's been a while, lover."

My veins run cold as his free hand gropes my breast. *No, no, no.*

He turns me around and pulls at my shirt while I fight to keep my arms down. Then he reaches in his pocket and out comes a box cutter. Effortlessly, he cuts the material from me.

I move to break away, but he pushes me to the living room floor. The old carpet is rough against the skin of my stomach.

His elbow comes down on the back of my head as he pins my face into the carpet. The box cutter blade flashes before he presses it to my cheek.

"Now, now, be still, Pamela. We wouldn't want to stain more carpet with your blood, would we?"

I fight the urge to vomit.

He straddles me, grinding his erection into my denim-covered ass. "Before we get to the fun stuff, I need to know where my boys are."

I say nothing. *Kill me, asshole, but I will not speak.*

He grabs my hair and lifts my head.

Wham! He slams my face into the floor. Pulling me back, he does it again and again. My nose cracks, and blood runs down onto my lips then pools on the old, worn carpet.

"Where are my boys, Pamela?"

Again, I say nothing, and he releases my head and moves the box cutter from my cheek down to my neck.

Flick.

The blade nicks my skin. It burns, and the air hitting the opening only makes it sting further.

He leans down. "I'm gonna check my marks. Better be still, or I'll give you more." He licks the wound on my neck before pushing off me. Then he slides my jeans and panties down.

My face throbs, blood is running down onto the carpet, my neck burns, and my ass is now exposed to him.

The slap comes before I can brace, surely leaving a handprint behind on my bare bottom. He trails the box cutter over my back and down my ass cheeks, making me aware that he's in charge, before he scoots my knees under me, spreading my pussy open. After he rubs his calloused fingers over the lips, feeling every raised circle he created, he laughs, and I dry heave.

"Feels good. Remember when I gave you these?"

Like it was fucking yesterday.

Tied to our bed, I'm immobile and exhausted. He has fucked me for hours. The little blue pill said to call the doctor if you have an erection lasting more than four hours, we have to be close to that mark now.

The smell of sex and cigarettes assaults my nose.

"Let's have some fun." He laughs his evil laugh that only lets me know I am in more trouble. "You're mine, Pamela. No one else's. I'm going to make sure everyone knows this pussy is used."

Before I can contemplate what he means, the cigarette comes down on my pussy lip, the cherry burning into my skin before extinguishing. I cry out in agony. I fight the ties on my wrists and ankles, only causing them to cut into my skin farther.

He blows the ash off my lips, offering no relief to the raw skin.

I brace myself, try to contain myself, as he relights the cigarette and does it again. Over and over, he burns marks into my lips.

The adrenaline finally leaves me limp, defeated.

Hell has a special place for men like him. He just can't seem to get there fast enough.

After he finally passed out that night, I soaked in a cold bath for an hour, trying to ease the pain between my legs. Using petroleum jelly diaper creams from the boys, I tried to minimize scarring, but the tissue was damaged. I healed, but the marks remained.

Everything with him has been one scar after another, whether physically or emotionally. He has left no part of me unbattered.

His fingers plunge inside me. "This can all be over. I'll stop if you tell me where my boys are. I know you wouldn't be far from them. I'll find them, Pamela. Tell me now and I'll stop."

I can only lie here and wish for a quick death. Let my boys be free. Let him never find them. I'll take their location to my grave.

I'm in agony with every touch.

My will is gone. He wins. He has finally broken me beyond repair. Those are my thoughts as I feel him enter me from behind.

I am done.

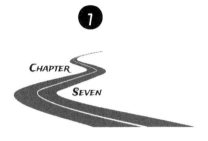

CHAPTER

SEVEN

BOOMER

*I*f she doesn't answer this door, I'm going to break *it down*, I think right before I hear movement.

It's a damn trailer. I could rip the shit off the hinges. What kind of game is she playing?

"Pamela, I'm not fuckin' around. You're gonna tell me what's going on. Open the door, dammit."

Shuffling, whimpering … She doesn't answer.

"Pamela, it's Shooter. Look, the club just wants to know you're okay. If you don't want Boomer here, at least talk to me. We're blind here, and that's a fucked up place to put us. Open the door or we open it. Last chance." Always the calm one, Shooter goes to his truck and comes back with a flat head screwdriver.

We hear the sound of the back door slamming, and Shooter takes off to the noise while I shove the flat head into the lock and pop it. I am met with the resistance of a chain, and looking inside, my heart stops.

Pamela is on the floor, face down, crawling to the couch to pull herself up. She is naked and bleeding from her face and neck.

I throw my shoulder into the door and the chain flies off. I rush to her.

Her swollen eyes meet mine, and she shakes her head back and forth as I approach.

"No, Boomer, fucking *no*!" she screams.

I drop to my knees, helpless in front of her.

There is nothing to humble a man and bring him to the brink more than seeing someone he cares about violated in the worst of ways. It's written all over her demeanor. How much has she endured?

"Pami, please." I drop my head into my hands. I need to touch her, to comfort her.

"You need to leave, Boomer," she says with each word cracking. "This isn't about you or your club." She moves around, getting dressed as I sit helplessly on my knees in her living room.

When I notice her blood stains the carpet in front of me, I break a little more inside.

"Pami, please let me help you."

"It's my burden to bear," she says, pulling on her pants and wrapping her cut shirt around her. "I need you to leave."

"Look at me," I whisper, hearing Shooter come back inside. He stands in the end of her small hallway, and I shake my head to get him to stay. The last thing I need is for her to get more spooked.

She finally looks at me.

"He's gonna die, baby. You need to know I'm gonna fuckin' kill him."

As tears fall down her face, she reaches out to touch my beard yet stops short. "Boomer, let it go. Let me go. This isn't your problem."

Her words are like a knife to my heart. For the first time in forever, I feel something, and she is rendering me helpless. Emotions well inside me, tears threatening to fall. I am a man, but I am not strong enough to watch her being hurt.

"Anybody give it to you better than me, Pami?" I ask her, knowing the answer. She told me time and time again and it wasn't just the orgasms.

"Boomer, let it go."

"You're mine, Pami. You've been mine since the

moment I breathed you in and you made my heart beat again. I've done bad things for stupid reasons. I've done good things for the wrong reasons. I've been to the edge of never and wondered why I was still breathing.

"You, I'm still breathing for you. My heart is still beating for you. As broken as I am, I am who I am for you. Call it fate, call it destiny, call it whatever the fuck you want, but I was made for you. I was made for this moment. Nothing in my life will ever compare to being able to bring you back from the brink. Pami, please, I'm begging." I let a tear fall. "Tell me what is going on and tell me who did it so they can pay, and baby, you can be safe."

She looks around as if she's looking for him, and once she sees Shooter, she stops.

"He's gone. Went out the back door, probably because he was outnumbered, fuckin' pussy."

Pamela slumps down onto the couch as if she has lost the world. Shooter doesn't move, and when I start to, he shakes his head at me.

"Been through this with Tessie, Pamela. You know that," Shooter says calmly. "I need you to breathe through it."

I look at Pamela who has paled in front of me, and I watch as she starts shaking. It kills me not to comfort her, not to hold her, not to be able to tell her and show her it's going to be all right. Somehow, some way, I will get her through this.

"Gotta breathe, Pamela. Inhale," Shooter tries to talk her down from the shock that is setting in. It's not working, and dammit to hell, I need to do something.

I move to the couch then pull her to me, and she screams out and beats on my chest.

"Shh … Pami … shhh. It's me, Boomer. Breathe, honey, breathe. You gotta breathe with me."

I take a deep breath as I hold her against me. It takes a moment, but she settles and begins to breathe with me. Then the sobs come, and I hold her through them. I don't care if I am here in this very spot for the next week; I will hold her through it all.

Shooter leans against the wall, typing a text, most likely to Doc Kelly so we can get Pamela checked out.

I rub my hand over her hair, feeling myself calming as she relaxes against me.

"He's gonna kill me," she whispers between crying hiccups. "He's gonna kill me this time."

The words slice into my soul … *this time*. What has this woman lived through? Who the hell is this man?

I swear on everything I believe in that I'm going

to make him pay. She will be free and safe from him if it's the last damn thing I do.

Pamela

I was sure I was going to die today. I was certain, once he finished fucking me, punishing me, I was going to die at the hands of my husband.

I sit up, pushing myself off Boomer, and promptly throw up all over my ugly, green carpet. Shame left the building the day Dennis burned his marks into my pussy.

I should care that Shooter and Boomer have found me in the worst way possible. I should care that I puked all over my floor without trying to get to the bathroom. I should care about a lot of things. I don't.

The only thing that matters is my sons are safe … for now. He hasn't found them. The level of violence he has resorted to today shows me he means me harm, and he doesn't know where they are. He probably thought I would cave.

He was wrong.

Shooter and Boomer showing up stopped him

from inflicting more damage, but there is no way I was giving up my sons, no matter what he did to me.

As if it happens every day, Shooter goes into the kitchen and comes back with paper towels to clean up my mess. He then brings me a cup of water while Boomer moves my hair from my face and sits me on his lap.

My body aches, but I don't have the energy to make a sound.

I want nothing more than a bath and to sleep. Then again, Dennis is probably watching, and the minute I'm alone again, he will come back and finish the job.

What happens then? Who helps my mom with my boys? How will she get by? How will they get by? What will they think of me? How will my mom get the news? Is she strong enough to handle that?

I look up to see Doll enter my house with a woman and a medical bag, and I freeze.

Boomer is right there, whispering in my ear. "It's gonna be all right. She's just gonna help clean you up."

Clean me up. There is no help for the mess I have made. He's talking about my broken nose and bloodied face. Sure, the good doctor can clean that, but who will clean up the mess of my life?

"I've got kids," I whisper to Boomer.

Desperation and fear do something to a woman. I can take any level of pain. I can take any level of abuse for my boys. I have to be smart, though. I have to think ahead. I have to give them a backup plan. I have no one … except the Hellions. I have to take the leap of faith that, after Dennis finishes with me, they will keep my boys safe.

"Figured that out by now, Pami."

"Boomer, I've got two boys—Wesson and Colt. He can't get to them. No matter what, he can't—"

"He's not, honey. He's not. On everything I am, I give you my word no one will get to them. We're gonna bring your boys home to you."

Tears roll down my face, and the salty liquid hits my busted nose and lips, making them burn.

"They can't come home. Promise me, Boomer. Keep them away. He's gonna kill me this time."

Boomer's grip on my hips tightens. "You aren't going anywhere except to pack a bag and stay with me. Then I'll get your boys home to you where they belong. This motherfucker will never lay another hand on you."

"He-he-he's gonna win. He already has," I sob.

"He is not, and he has not! Trust me, Pamela. Trust me with your boys."

"They are living in a church parsonage at the coast," I whisper, swallowing down the lump in my throat. "My mom has them at a small home meant for the pastor of the church in Stella."

Boomer glances at Shooter. "Call Tripp. Call a sermon. She's my ol' lady; those are my kids. Figure that shit out."

"She's yours?" Doll questions Boomer, watching me.

"That's what I said. You want it in blood? I'll give it to you. Those boys are mine; she's mine. Now can we handle it?" Boomer drops his voice, trying to contain his emotions while Doll takes in the two of us.

"Your boys are in Stella, you said?"

After I nod, not understanding, the tiny blonde bites her bottom lip and makes a call.

"Daddy, we need you." That simple sentence changes my entire world before I can blink.

She gets off the phone after sharing only the information of where my boys are and who my mother is.

"Roundman and the Haywood's Landing Hellions will have your mom and boys on our compound within the hour. No one can get to them there." Doll smiles proudly. "Can we get Doc Kelly to give you a once-over, please? Just to make me feel better."

I don't move. I can't.

"Pamela, you're a Hellion. Stella is so close to my dad they could walk to the church and get them if they wanted to. This is what families do. Please know my dad will lay down his life and every other patched member before they let anything happen to your mom and sons. I give you my word."

"How?" I ask, not understanding why they would want to help me.

"Are you Boomer's ol' lady?" Doll asks, smiling.

"Damn right she is," Boomer barks out before I can answer.

"So, last I checked, Boomer wears the cut; he earned his patch. He's a Hellion, and you're his woman. Ride or die, this is what we do … together."

She makes it sound so simple, yet I know it's so much more than that.

When she reaches out her small hand to me, I hesitate. I have been alone and afraid for so long. Is this the answer to my prayers? Is this the way to be with my boys again?

I look over at Boomer, and with shaking hands, I cup his face, running my thumbs over his beard. "I've got kids, Boomer. I've got baggage by the boatloads. I don't know how I feel about men after Dennis. I have scars on the inside and the out. Why are you taking this on?"

He looks at me, his brown eyes meeting my gaze, and there is no reservation in them, only determination. "No kid should be without their momma when they have a strong as steel Momma like you. No woman should be broken by the hands or words of a man.

"I've got my own baggage, Pami. I have scars on the inside and the out. I just want a chance to show you and your kids what it is to be free. I've spent my whole life seeking the freedom to be. While I've dedicated years to training and fought in wars in the name of giving freedom, I've never felt free for one moment of my life except when I'm with you.

"No matter what the future holds, you're mine and your kids are mine to protect and treasure. I just want the chance to give you freedom. I just want the chance for you simply to be you. Can I have that?"

I nod my head, feeling every bit a part of a family for the first time since my childhood.

"I had a good Mom, Pami, the best. Lost her way too young. She taught me right from wrong. I haven't always done right, but I promise you I'll do right by you and your boys."

I smile and lean against him as he wraps his arms

around me. I am safe and free in his arms. I exhale, and for the first time in years, I think I might just live. I might really have a life with my kids.

Boomer gave me that hope. Boomer is giving me the chance to simply be me. My mom, my kids, and Boomer, we can simply be.

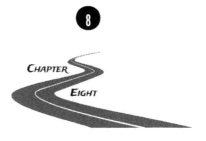

BOOMER

W e arranged a call to her mother so she was aware Roundman and the Haywood's Hellions were coming for them. In all the pain she endured today, there was a peace in her once she knew they would be protected.

Once that was all settled, Doc Kelly checked her out, and although her nose may need to be reset, she will heal from all the damage he inflicted. Mentally and emotionally, she may never truly recover, but physically, she is a survivor.

Since she never actually planned to stay and

hadn't acquired a bunch of junk, we packed up her belongings relatively quickly, and now we are in my home where she just finished her fifth shower and getting ready for bed. I have a feeling she will shower five more times tonight, but I don't care—whatever makes her keep pushing through.

I grab a pillow from the bed and make my way to the couch. My couch isn't the best, but it will damn sure beat sleeping on the floor tonight.

I never thought about the size of my house before. However, with Pamela and two kids here where I have only one bedroom and one bathroom, I see construction in my future.

"Boomer," she whispers.

"Yeah, Pami?" I turn, looking over my shoulder at her.

"I don't want to sleep alone. I need to know I'm not alone."

Without hesitating, I make my way over to her. I toss the pillow back in its spot and climb in. I then pull her to me like I have so many times before. She fits against me as if it's second nature, and for this moment, all is right with the world.

Almost.

I do believe that children who have a mom with as much heart as Pamela should be with her, not away from her. There are kids out there with mothers who don't care, and they are stuck with them, like it or not. Then you have Pamela's situation that feels almost helpless.

How is it that the bitches seem to have all the luck, while the good women get held down?

She sighs against me. "I messed up, Boomer. I messed it all up for my kids."

"No, Pami, you did the best you could for them."

"Do you believe in angels?"

"I'd like to think that my momma can see the man she raised. I'd like to think she is watching over me."

"I had a daughter, Boomer." She pauses, holding back emotions. "Cannon was their little sister. He hit me one too many times in the stomach that night, and I hit my head and blacked out. When I came to, the contractions were too close together. I didn't make it in time to stop them. I didn't buy my baby girl enough time."

I stroke her hair as her pain fills my chest. The loss, the guilt, the sadness, I feel it all. I know the emotions all too well.

"Boomer, no matter what happens, I gave my boys time. I failed their sister, but I bought them time away from him."

"Quit talking like he's gonna get you. I'm not gonna let that happen, Pamela. Believe that."

"You ever wish you could turn back the hands of time? Even though you got something good in the end, you ever wish you could go back?"

I continue to stroke her hair and try not to let the moisture soaking my T-shirt kill me. Although I want to take away her pain, I learned a long time ago that no one can do that. People can come along and ease the ache, but no one can take it away.

I murmur without actually answering. Do I wish I could go back? With every breath I take. I wish I could go back and switch places with my now dead brother-in-arms. He had so much to live for. Me, I had a mom in the grave and no family left to worry for. I had friends, sure, but they could move on. Skid, however, had a wife and a baby on the way.

"My boys are the best thing that ever happened to me. As much as I love them, I love them enough to let them go. If I could turn back time, I never would have been with him. I never would have met Dennis Williams. I know that would mean I wouldn't have my boys, and the thought of that …" She pauses in an attempt to control her emotions. "It kills me, but Boomer, if I could turn back time, I would because this isn't the life I ever wanted to give them."

The nagging question I shouldn't ask pops out. "Why stay for as long as you did?"

She moves, and I tighten my grip around her. I don't want her to run. I want to get to the real Pamela, the one who is vulnerable, the one who is beautiful, the one who is the strongest woman I have ever known.

"I was young, dumb, and once upon a time, I was in love, or so I thought."

"You don't believe anymore?" I ask after hearing her defeated tone.

"I believe people aren't always who you think they are. I believe that the sum of one plus one isn't always two."

"What does that mean?"

"Boomer, if you meet someone and have a connection, you build on that connection, right?"

I nod my head but don't speak.

"You let your walls down, but you also dream. You allow yourself to dream of a future. Then, somewhere along the way, the fantasy is nowhere near the reality. The person you thought you knew is long gone, and in their place is a stranger and, in some instances, a monster.

"One plus one in my marriage didn't make two. Everything was his way, his time, and his terms.

There was no part of me allowed to be free. Instead of coming together to multiply, he divided. He divided me into tiny, little pieces of myself that I don't think will ever be whole again."

"Take back the power, Pami. Take back your life," I whisper, feeling her loss.

"He's never gonna let me live with my boys without him. How can I take back anything when my entire body reminds me of him? He marked me from the inside out. Every day, I wake up and fight the pull to style my hair the way he liked it. I dress purposely, showing off my body, because he would want me covered."

"The tattoo?"

"Imagine having a scar you have to feel every time you go to the bathroom—a constant reminder of him, a constant reminder that, if I didn't give him what he wanted, when he wanted it, I would pay … painfully. I tried to cover it up. I tried to turn something bad into something beautiful."

I kiss the top of her forehead. "Most beautiful pussy I've ever seen. Most passionate pussy I've ever had. More than that, it's part of the strongest woman I've ever known. We'll get through this."

And we will. If it's the only thing I get right in

this life, I'm going to give Pami the opportunity to live her life free of him.

Pamela

Boomer lets me cry on his chest while stroking my hair and giving me the security that nothing can get to me right now. I have this moment. I have this time to get it all out. Oh, how I wish I could believe him. Oh, how I wish I could live in the bubble of Boomer's safety. I know Dennis, though. He will keep on until he kills me while trying to get me to talk. I won't, though.

Wesson and Colt are the only things I have gotten right in this world. I may have messed them up, but they are the good in me. I won't give up on making sure they are free from the monster.

I will die before he gets to my boys again. I have made peace with my mistakes—him being the biggest one I ever made. If sacrificing my life for my boys to be away from him is what it takes, I will gladly pull the trigger myself.

My body aches from Dennis, and my heart hurts, but my mind is suddenly focused.

It's going to be me or him, no way around it.

I have never been the violent type. Growing up, I was Suzy fucking sunshine … until Dennis. He took all my joy away until he gave me my kids. Then he took her away, my baby Cannon. All this time, year after year, I have allowed myself to be beaten and broken at his hands.

No more.

They say anger is a healthy part of the grieving process.

I don't feel anger. No, I feel fury.

I am furious for the joy he stole. I am furious for the years he's taken from me. I am furious for the childhood innocence my children never experienced. Allowing your children to be free to be kids is the gift we give them; only, Dennis didn't do that. No, he ripped that away the first time he hit me in front of them.

He made my children feel helpless. He made me feel weak.

Well, helpless, I am not, and weak, I am no more!

Dennis Williams has touched me for the last time. He will not get a chance again. I will kill him myself before he finds my boys or gets his fingers on my body.

I dry my tears and settle against Boomer. What a

mess I have brought him into. I need to get away from him, too.

I won't ruin anyone else's life with my problems. I appreciate the Haywood's Hellions helping my mom and boys. It's not their problem, though. I can't expect a club to take in my family as their own.

Who am I? Nothing but a whore who made her place on her back. Once I stop, will they put my mom and kids out? Did I make my mess even bigger now? What will happen to my mom and kids if I disappear to regroup until Dennis finds me again?

On one hand, I want to face him and put a bullet in him. Of course, that means jail. Mom would be free with my kids, though. On the other hand, I had this much time with the boys safe, and I could do it again. I will move west, and he will follow me. The more distance between my kids and me, the better they are, even if it breaks my heart into a million pieces.

"You're a million miles away," Boomer whispers, reminding me he is still awake.

"Trying to sleep," I reply on a sigh.

"Trying to make a plan."

How does he know?

"Been a long day, Boomer," I reply honestly.

"Yeah, and a woman like you who loves her kids with every breath isn't allowing herself to face what happened today; instead, she's thinking ahead for her kids."

I say nothing. What can I say? He's right.

"I've been through this with Shooter and Tessie, remember? Tessie would have lost her shit if she didn't have Axel to keep her going. You let Wesson and Colt be your reason to keep going, honey. They need their momma."

"Do they really?" I don't see how they do when I make a mess of everything.

"As a grown-ass man who misses his momma, yes, honey, they do."

"Boomer …" I start, sitting up to look him in the eyes.

"Yeah, honey?"

"How are you so confident, so sure of yourself? More than that, how are you even remotely okay with me and all my baggage?"

He smiles, and I want nothing more than to feel his beard against my face.

"I've seen a lot of shit, Pami, shit I wish I hadn't. I've done a lot of shit, a lot I wish I hadn't. I've felt loss that cuts so deeply the wound will never heal. The only good I've ever had outside of when my momma was alive has been with you."

"It's sex, Boomer."

His eyes never leave mine. "Keep tellin' yourself that, but it's always been more with us, and you know it. The minute you quit lying to yourself about everything is the minute you can finally start sorting your life for real. No running, no hiding, but really facing and fixing it. You gotta get real with yourself and everyone around you."

"I am real with myself. I'm a barfly. My job—" He cuts me off.

"You get paid to fuck me? You get paid to suck my dick so hard I see stars? Last I checked, Pami, you get paid to clean houses and a few offices."

"Boomer, you know I don't get paid, but I get a place. There have been more than just you ..." I pause, not wanting to hurt his feelings.

"I'm very aware there have been more than me, but I happen to know you give me more than them. Again, be real with yourself. You know what we have is more. It may not be roses and sunshine, and it damn sure isn't conventional, but it's something."

"I can't—"

"Or won't?"

Okay, mister, I will get real with myself.

"I won't!" When I start to push off him, his hand on my back remains firm, though it doesn't push me into him. If I want to get away from him, he's not going to stop me. He's simply reminding me he's here.

"Pami, you're going through hell. I don't expect you to commit and fall in love. I just want you to know I'm with you. Ride it out together. Whatever the future holds, we'll face it together. See the word 'together,' it means not alone. When I came to the Hellions, I was no longer riding alone. When you came to the Hellions, even as a barfly, you weren't alone anymore."

"It's not that simple," I argue.

"Sure it is. Make the choice to let it be. Let me help you and your boys. Whatever happens, we deal with it together."

Can it be this easy? Can I let Boomer and the Hellions take on my mess? I did this to myself and my kids, so why would they be willing to go to bat for trash like me?

Boomer watches me closely, and I drop my head back onto his chest to avoid his knowing stare.

"Don't over-think it all. Just give me and the club a chance to help you, to show you it's going to be okay, and to protect you."

"What—"

"What nothing. Ride with me. Ride it out with my club. Simple enough. When the dust settles, we'll figure out the future together. Don't complicate everything; just be with me." He kisses the top of my head, his beard tickling my forehead.

The simple touch eases my anxiety. He is a like a balm to my sensitive skin. He is a salve to my wounds, slowly healing little parts of me at a time.

Can it be this simple? Ride with Boomer and let the club help me get my family safe? Can I have the hope to have a life with my kids again?

CHAPTER NINE

BOOMER

I should have known there would be no sleep tonight. After hours of sharing and finally exhaustion winning, Pami is sound asleep on me.

Never one to sleep heavily without medication after all my years in the service, I am alert when I hear the breaking glass of my back door. I slide my hand between my mattresses to get my Glock.

"Pami," I whisper and nudge her awake.

She sleepily pushes off me.

"Crawl to the closet, baby, and stay put. No matter what you hear, you stay in the closet."

The problem with a one bedroom cabin is there isn't a whole lot of space to not only hide someone, but to get them secure before an intruder makes their way to you.

I hear the door open, and Pami freezes over me.

"Pami, move slowly and crawl under the bed."

She stills, and I nudge her into action. Once she is off me and moving to the side of the bed, I get up and move to the doorway.

Standing in the dark against the wall, I control my breathing and watch for the shadow to make its way into the room. Except, the cocky son of a bitch stops right outside the doorway.

"Pamela, I'm coming for you."

At his voice, Pamela jumps up from the side of the bed where she was secure. Her eyes go wide as he enters the space with a gun pointed right at her.

You've got to be fucking kidding me! I want to roar, but I have to remain in control.

His hand is steady, his arm firm, aiming the gun right at the chest of the mother of his children.

"Where are my boys, bitch?"

"Where you'll never get to them," Pami states firmly, almost goading him.

I wait for the jackass to look around to see me. I

wait for him to try to turn on the light. He certainly can't be stupid enough to think she's here alone.

I keep my breathing even and remain silent and still. The last thing I want to do is spook him and have Pami end up with a bullet wound … or worse.

"Your friend"—he pauses as if thinking—"what's her name? Oh, yeah, your friend Keri was helpful in locating you."

This has my attention.

"I don't have a friend named Keri," Pami says boldly. She doesn't move, yet she isn't backing down. "Stop the games, Dennis. If you wanna shoot me, do it. I'm not telling you where the boys are. I'll die first."

He laughs menacingly. "You'll die when I'm ready for you to die. Never could understand, could you, Pamela? You are mine to do with as I please. I marked you."

"You scarred me," she fires back.

"Yep, and those marks are how I found you. A craigslist add for a special dotted pussy was quickly answered with 'I have a friend with a tattooed pussy.' " He laughs harshly. "A little money incentive, a sob story of a husband with a wife who ran off after going through the loss of a child, and I had your where-abouts and a new friend. I think it's sweet you prettied up my design. A butterfly, though … I didn't peg you as the delicate kind."

"You don't know a damn thing about me."

"I know you're gonna tell me where my boys are," he commands.

"I'll die first."

At his twitch, I react, moving quickly out of the shadows. Once at his side, I hold my gun to his temple.

"I've killed people for no reason except to follow an order before, so killing you will be nothing on the list of reasons I'm going to Hell."

He moves, and Pamela drops to the floor just as the gun goes off.

I pull the trigger without hesitation.

Pamela screams yet remains on the floor on the other side of the bed.

His blood splatters all over my wall along with brain matter as his body drops and his gun slips from his grasp.

I wipe my face and blink. Blank. Void. Black. I have to numb myself to the situation. I took another life.

I hear her crying but refrain from moving to her.

"Pamela, I need you to call the police," I say calmly without going to her.

She has truly seen me at my worst now. She knows what I am capable of. It's over now. No turning back.

I watch her sit on her knees on my floor and reach for her phone. She rattles off our situation and location to the dispatcher in a panic. The dispatcher must have asked her about me because she looks to me with tears rolling down her face and states perfectly, "No, I'm not in any danger anymore. Boomer saved me."

My chest aches with the pull to touch her, to hold her. I can't, though. I took another man's life. Regardless of the reason, I killed another man. I killed her husband. I killed the father of her children. She will never get beyond tonight.

I don't know if I will ever move on. I reacted. Did I react wrong? Would he really have killed Pamela? I guess we will never know. I wasn't willing to risk it, though. I hesitated long enough for him to fire one round, and that was one round too many.

My mind goes to the place I shouldn't let it … What if Pamela hadn't moved? What if the bullet had hit its mark?

I stand still in the dark of my room with the woman who has captured my mind sitting huddled by my bed, crying while her husband bleeds out on my floor.

Claim her, give her the protection of the club, and give her life with her kids—it was supposed to be simple. Only, now can it ever be? Will she forever be haunted by the events that happened right in front of her? Will she ever see me as the man who could bring her body to life and keep her safe? Or will I always be the killer who took out her husband?

Bile builds in my throat, and I swallow hard not to puke. Man up, they always say. Boys are trained from a young age to steel their emotions. Don't run and cry into your mom's apron; be a man.

Well, I don't want to cry, and I have no remorse for the scumbag being dead, but I do feel bad that Pamela had to witness this side of me, the side that will do anything to protect the people who matter to me.

I have lost enough in my life helplessly. Tonight, I wasn't going to lose her at the hands of a dickhead.

I am who I am. I have no regrets about using my skills to keep her alive for her boys. I just hope she can still accept me as I am.

Pamela

The paramedics come in, and the body bag goes out, carrying Dennis. The police have taken our statements. Boomer is not being arrested right now, but he's not to leave town without notifying them until the case is closed.

Dennis is dead.

The man who has been my source of torture, pain, and heartache for so many years is gone. I can go to my kids and no longer look over my shoulder.

Elation runs through me. Then I look over to Boomer whose eyes are hiding a pain so deep.

Guilt?

Sorrow hits me like a punch to the gut. He took a man's life to save mine. Does he feel bad?

We are in his living room, and he keeps looking to his bedroom door, the room that may not have a body left in it, but still has the mess that shooting someone in the head leaves behind.

Boomer doesn't speak as the last of the patrol cars pulls out of the driveway. He moves to the room, his room, and I decide to give him space.

When he emerges a little while later, he has showered and changed. No doubt, he wanted to feel clean.

Even though he had to change and give his clothes to the police, he didn't get to shower until now.

I notice he has my bag in his hand.

Well, this is it.

I steel myself. My problems are over, so it's time to send me packing. It's okay. I can do this. I can get on the road and get to my kids. I have some money saved. Mom, my boys, and I can have a fresh start.

All that together talk was Boomer's way of supporting me while I was in trouble. Now it's time to be on my own. I got into this mess on my own, and I will walk away alone. That is how it should be.

I will forever treasure my time with him. Nathan 'Boomer' Vaughn has given me the best moments of my adult life outside of holding my children for the first time. He gave me little memories all for myself. Now it's time to be 'Mom' again, and I need to focus my attention on Wesson and Colt, anyway.

I don't speak as he walks over and takes me by the hand. He guides us out without speaking and doesn't bother locking his house.

"Boomer, you should lock the door," I remind him, thinking maybe tonight has been too much for him.

"Honey, the only person stupid enough to break into the house of an Army Green Beret is your husband, and how did that work out for him?" His eyes grow wide, and his tone is sharp. "I've got nothing real valuable inside that house, because I live in the woods and know how to hide my valuables better than that. The gun I keep inside is now in a bag on its way to the police evidence locker. I have a side arm in the glove box of my truck.

"We're going to a hotel because we need to sleep, and I don't know about you, but I don't feel like cleaning up the mess in my bedroom right now. My couch is shit, and the jackass broke the glass on my back door, so the house isn't secure even if I do lock it. So let's go get some sleep and tackle what happens next in the morning, okay?"

"Sleep, as in, together? You're staying with me?"

"Unless you need space, yeah, we're going to sleep. If you want more, that's on you. With everything you've been through, you don't have to, and that's okay, too. Right now, I wanna take us to get some sleep so we can clear our heads safely then get you to your boys tomorrow."

My boys … tomorrow. With all the craziness and the many emotions running through me, this is the light at the end of a very dark tunnel. I can hold my boys tomorrow.

"You're gonna go with me?"

His eyes flash with something I can't read. "As long as you want me around, I'm there. If you want me gone, once I get you to them, I'm gone."

He makes it sound so simple. He killed a man protecting me, yet he is willing to walk away if I want him to.

I put the back of my hand to my forehead. I don't have a fever. I'm not delirious. I pinch my arm. I'm not dreaming.

My husband is dead. Boomer gave me that escape, whether that was his original intention or not. Push came to shove, and it was save me or let Dennis shoot. Boomer chose me. Now, if I say the word, he walks away.

I have never had control or power over my situation before. Boomer gives me that. If I want more, I can have it. If I don't, he walks. Simple as that.

"Come on, Pami. Let's get out of here and try to get some sleep. You need your head clear to figure out your future."

I nod and follow him to his truck. We go to town and get a room at the local hotel. It's nothing fancy, but it is a shower, a bed, and a place that doesn't have remnants of my husband on the walls.

I close my eyes and breathe deeply. One step at a

time, I will get beyond this. It's over. I can breathe. No more looking over my shoulder.

Today is like a birthday. Today is the first day of the rest of my life. No matter how many times Dennis has hurt me over the years, I get to have my boys now. I get to have my life without him.

My boys won't live their lives worrying about their mom. They will get to have me with them every day.

Tomorrow.

I watch as Boomer cautiously moves around the room. He doesn't touch me. He is giving me space. I need space. I need to process this.

My husband is dead. The monster is gone. He can't get to me.

Boomer shrugs out of his jeans and T-shirt, stripping down to just his boxer briefs. Earlier, he wore sweats and a T-shirt to bed for my comfort. Since the hotel has two beds, I guess he assumes we are sleeping alone.

I watch as the Hellions' insignia tattoo on his back moves with him. His shoulder has a tattoo of a tombstone with a gun and soldier's helmet.

I fight my pull to run my fingers over each design covering his chest and, instead, move to my bag and get my pajamas out. Okay, my oversized T-shirt that I love to sleep in since formal pajamas cost more than a clearance man's shirt.

Brushing my teeth, I try to make my mind stop spinning with thoughts of the future. I have to find a job, get a new place for my mom and boys. We are from Virginia; does Mom want to go back there? Do we start completely fresh somewhere?

I hear Boomer shifting on the old bed, bringing me back to the moment.

I finish cleaning up, thinking about the man in the room with me. If it wasn't for the man in there, I wouldn't be able to think of a future with my boys. No matter what happens, I owe my future to him.

I will never forget that this man saved my life and gave me a future full of hope when I was in a hopeless situation. I will never forget that he made the sacrifice of himself and how he will handle the rest of his life knowing he killed a man. Whether defending me or not, I know it has to be weighing on him. He sacrificed that to keep me breathing for my boys.

Without over-thinking, I crawl into the same bed as Boomer. In his arms, everything is finally right in my life.

No matter what happens, he gave me that, too: simple security, simple moments of peace, even if they are brief. He has given me simple safety.

10

CHAPTER TEN

BOOMER

I wasn't expecting her to sleep with me, and having her in my arms is a double-edged sword. It cuts deep. I want to hold her close, but I need to let her go.

I don't think the reality has hit her yet.

I killed her husband.

Will that forever stand between us? I feel the urge to take off on my bike and ride again. I need to hit the open road and not look back. I need to get Pamela to her boys and let them build their lives without the shadow of Dennis Williams and his killer.

I know I'm not going to be charged with anything. It was self-defense. All the justification in the world doesn't change that her husband died by my hand, though.

One shot, one kill, I have been trained. Take out any threat without hesitation. I am the machine I was built to be. There is no changing that. I need to accept all that I have done and find a way to make peace.

In all these years, I haven't found a way yet. One can only hope the day will come.

A man shouldn't feel all these emotions. We are taught that at a young age. Well, I feel every bit of the pain from taking a life. Regardless of Dennis Williams being a piece of shit, wife-beating asshole, I took away any possibility of change.

Would Pamela have wanted him to change? Will she wake up one day and wish Dennis had the chance to right his wrongs? Will she hate me for taking any hope away?

"Thinking awfully hard over there," Pamela says, waking from the other bed.

I have been up for hours, dressed, and sitting on the edge of the other full bed in the hotel. I didn't want to wake her. Any sleep she can get, she needs to take. I'm sure the weight of everything will hit soon enough, and the memories will haunt her for who knows how long.

"You wanna try to sleep a little more or hit the road to the coast?"

She smiles at me, and I memorize this moment: her hair wild around her face, her brown eyes dancing in excitement, and a mother's love shining in her features.

"I'm ready to get to my boys."

"What the lady wants …" I try to smile at her.

She looks down at the bedspread shyly. "You're the only man who has ever treated me like a lady."

"Umm, Pamela, don't twist who I am in your mind. Our relationship, or whatever the fuck you call it, hasn't been about you being a lady and me being a gentleman."

"Boomer, half the Hellions treat barflies like hookers, but you never did that with me. You're the only one who made sure I got mine"—she blushes, avoiding looking up—"before getting yours. You made sure I had dinner or breakfast. You made sure my car was running." She waves her arm in the air dramatically. "Before everything came out, you treated me like I was normal and that we had something more than orgasms between us. You talked to me, Boomer. You cared about my day even if you weren't getting laid that night. You randomly checked on me. You, Boomer Vaughn, treated me better than anyone has in my entire life."

"I'm no gentleman," I remind her. *Hello, I killed her husband less than twelve hours ago.*

"Yeah, Tripp says that, too, and Doll is over the moon happy and in love. Boomer, you give me something to believe in. You give me hope when I'm hopeless. I don't know what the future holds, but I need you in my life."

I smile at her as her words soothe my insecurities. "What the lady wants …"

"Good to know." She winks. "Can we go to my boys now?"

———

Haywood's Landing is a small town not far off the Crystal Coast of North Carolina. With Croatan National Forest nearby and the closest actual city being ten minutes away, it is a perfect, little place for a group of bikers to have their club, their businesses, and keep their families safe.

Roundman, Danza, Frisco, and Rocky really thought through all the details of building a brotherhood so many years ago. Not only have the Hellions supported each other through the good, the bad, and the times one of our brothers is locked up, they have created a family where blood isn't thicker than water, but one where brotherhood comes before everything. They have created a brotherhood of total acceptance, a family where no one is ever alone, a safe haven for less than perfect people to feel like they can have hope for something real again. It's simple: once a Hellion, always a Hellion, and we have each other's backs. Whether you agree with a brother or not, you take his back, as he will yours.

Family. We ride together, we die together.

Our destination is a small, three bedroom, two bathroom doublewide not far from the compound. Ruben 'Ruby' Castillo and his wife Jenna 'Vida' Natera de Castillo de Natera have taken in Pamela's mom and sons. I'm sure things are crowded since they have three kids of their own, but Vida is the perfect person to take in the boys and grandma. I don't know them well, but I know they have been together since back when they lived in Mexico, and Jenna is a dedicated wife and mother.

Pulling up, I sigh. This is it—time to let her go. If only it were that simple...

"They have a black picket fence?" Pamela says, as if she doesn't understand.

I let out a small laugh. "Jenna, being from Mexico, always wanted a picket fence in her yard. Ruby gave her that. Then Jenna took over for Doll in the office when she got with Tripp, and after she befriended Doll and Sass, they said they weren't white picket fence women, so they gave it a Hellions' makeover and painted it black."

She giggles and sighs. "This is what normal is?"

"I don't know, honey. Never had normal." I run my hand over my beard.

"Black picket fences, I can handle that."

"Let's go see your boys." I hop out of the truck and make my way to the front to open her door; only, she is already out and coming to me.

It's time to give her … normal. Her new normal. Her safe normal. Pamela is going to have what she and her boys should have had years ago …

A life together.

I make it to the bottom step of the front porch before my two boys barrel out the door and into my arms. I step back to take their weight as each one latches on.

"Momma," Wesson cries out, and it's music to my ears and heaven in my heart.

Full.

For the first time in over a year, I feel full again with my boys in my arms and my mother's tear-filled face looking over me. My family.

Boomer stands behind me, giving us this time. My boys, my mom, and maybe one day, my man all around me. I can't think about Boomer and the future with him right now, though. The two precious boys in my arms are my focus.

"Momma, we have friends. Ms. Vida and Mr. Ruby, they have kids—two girls and a boy. We've been having fun. I don't know why we left the other house. Memaw hasn't had to cook since we got here. Ms. Vida, she makes good food."

"A little hot," Colt adds with a smile.

"It's still good, though." Wesson nudges his brother as if he needs to get with the program.

Colt tugs on my shirt. "Momma, Mr. Ruby and his brothers—well, they say that, but they don't look nothin' alike," he rambles with his eyes wide. "They ride motor bikes. They are loud." He smiles excitedly, and I feel a moment of peace. My boys seem untouched by the whole mess I have put them through.

Tasting the salt of my own tears as they pass my lips, I inhale deeply. I have my boys back with me, and I don't have to look over my shoulder. I don't have to go to the gas station and buy a prepaid phone to make one random call after another. I don't have to mail my mother cash in untracked envelopes, sending a prayer she will get them. I can simply be with my family.

Relief consumes me from the bottom of my toes to the tippy top of my head. I can simply be.

A beautiful, Hispanic woman with long, black hair braided and hanging over her shoulder comes to the doorway. "Please come inside."

I step into the doublewide, and immediately, the feeling of home washes over me. We enter into the living room, which has a brown sectional sofa with no tables, but a rug with streets to play cars on is in the middle of the floor. To the side of the entertainment center is a cube shelf thing with bins of toys. Looking beyond the living area is a bar that opens to the kitchen. The white countertops and wood cabinets are like every other manufactured home I have been in. What covers each cabinet door is what brings my heart joy.

On each and every one is a drawing, painting, or school paper from her children.

I can do this. In my next home, I can cover every available inch with pieces of my children. I don't have to hide who I am anymore. Who we are doesn't have to be a secret.

"Vida," I hear a man yell from another room, "I'm hungry."

"He's always hungry." The Hispanic woman smiles at me. "I'm Jenna, and this is our home." She extends her hand in greeting.

When I reach out, she pulls me into a hug, surprising me.

"Come in and get comfortable. I'm making green chicken enchiladas for dinner. I hope you're hungry."

"Oh, love, she cooks amazing," my mom whispers beside me as she rubs her belly. "I've gained at least five pounds being here in, like, a day." My mother laughs, and my heart feels like it will burst. When was the last time either of us could relax?

It was before Dennis Williams. That is the last moment of peace I have had, and as my mother, I am sure she knew and was in knots over it.

A man comes from the back and embraces Boomer in a manly half-hug backslap. He wears a leather vest like Boomer with patches. Boomer is around six-foot tall, and this man is just as tall with dark hair slicked back and a tattoo under his eye of what I think is supposed to be a diamond.

"Ruby," he says, turning to me and extending his hand.

I shake it and notice his knuckles have the word 'Vida' inked across them as he pulls away.

What is it like to have a man who is that devoted?

He walks to his wife and immediately kisses her passionately without a care in the world that he has a house full of people and kids around.

"I'm hungry," he growls then whispers in her ear, making her blush.

"Dinner will be ready soon." She pulls away and moves to the kitchen. She looks over her shoulder at me. "Make yourself at home. Your mom and boys have been staying in my Maritza's room. We don't have a lot of space, but what we have is yours as long as you need it."

I take it all in. Minute by minute, second by second, I soak it all up: sitting down to a meal with my sons, getting them ready for bed, reading to them, and then lying down for night time snuggles.

Lying on the floor—Wesson asleep on my right, Colt on my left—we are all together in a bed made of blankets. This is the best moment of my life, outside of their births. I look to the ceiling, at whoever has shined their light on me.

"Thank you," I whisper to the angels above.

I could have read for hours, but I stopped once I was two books beyond their steadied breathing. So what if they were out like a light? I could freely read to my boys, so I did. Tugging on their pajamas, I note I need to find a job quickly since these two have had a big growth spurt since I left them a year ago.

Pain fills me and I push it down.

No looking back. I have to focus forward. I can't think of the time I lost with them. I have to live in the joy that I have a future with them now. It wasn't promised, and two days ago, I never thought it would come, yet here I am.

I walked through hell and found my way through. I hit rock bottom and climbed my way up from the depths of despair.

I sigh and squeeze my boys closer to me. I have everything I need right here, right now, and I'm free to simply be.

I don't sleep. Instead, I count their breaths and count my blessings to be here with them once again.

When Dennis found me, I didn't think I would see them ever again. I made peace with giving up my life to give them a future. Now here we are, all together.

The next morning, I get up to find Boomer slept down the road at the Hellions' compound. Apparently, they have little apartments there for the guys. I am a little on edge that he left us, but it's obviously with people he trusts.

Vida is making omelets with Ruby's arms wrapped around her from behind as he whispers in her ear. She smiles, and I feel the love they share.

That is what I wanted for my boys. I wanted my kids to have a home where their dad loved me so much he couldn't take his eyes off me, didn't want to keep his hands off me—in a loving way—and there would be no angry disputes. I wanted a house full of love.

Ruby and Vida have made that for their kids, RJ (Ruben Jr), Mariella, and Maritza. They have given them a foundation made of love and loyalty.

My sons didn't get that start in life, but they will know, without a doubt, their mom and grandma will give anything to keep them safe. They will know the love we have for them. Most of all, I'm going to show them that, even when we are broken, we are not defeated, and we will fight to thrive again.

Never give up and never give in.

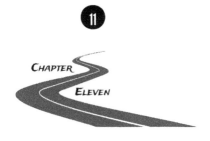

Six Months Later

BOOMER

I f I thought moving on was hell before, nothing
compares to knowing you have feelings for
someone, but you are no good in their life.

Pamela is doing well in Haywood's Landing.

I should be happy about this.

Should be …

She has a job at the garage where Roundman and

the guys look out for her and give her a steady paycheck. Ruby and Vida got her set up in a doublewide three doors down. She has set it up nicely for her mom, her, and the boys.

Colt started kindergarten alongside Wesson. With them being in hiding last year, they held the oldest back. It was smart.

Things are good for her, so why do I feel the loss? It's not like we had some long-standing love affair.

She had so many secrets; did I really ever know the real Pami? I would like to think I did. I would like to think we had a connection. Was it love? I don't know. Our circumstances weren't conducive to allowing us to find out.

Now the time for that has passed.

I tip the longneck bottle to Corinne so she knows I need another as the front door to Ruthless opens, and I hear one of my brothers telling someone to get out. Looking to the left, I see red.

"Keri, you were warned," I say as she moves toward me.

"Boomer, let me explain."

"You betrayed Pamela. Nothing to explain."

"It wasn't like that. He sucked me into his story. I thought he cared. I thought she had postpartum depression and ran away." She looks down. "I've been down the rabbit hole, Boomer. I know the pain of loss. I have secrets, too."

"I don't give a shit, Keri. The club doesn't give a shit. Loyalty, look it up. Your secrets might have mattered one day. Your pain might have mattered, too, but the moment you gave up any information on anyone even associated with the Hellions, you lost that. Lick your wounds somewhere else and learn your lesson."

"I messed up. It all worked out, though."

"All worked out!" I yell, pushing off the bar stool. "Pamela was almost shot by the father of her children. How the fuck do you think that worked out, woman?"

Corinne comes around from behind the bar. "Time to go, ho." She pushes on Keri's shoulders.

Keri slaps Corinne's arms away. "Get your hands off me!"

"Nah," Corinne says with a smirk. "See, these boys won't put their hands on a woman, but me … I wanna get you out front and beat the *shit* out of you."

"W-what?" Keri stammers.

"You gave up Pamela. You put her in danger. It wasn't your business. We've all got issues, Keri." Corinne waves her hands wildly through the air. "Not one person is innocent in life, but even if their only mistake is a white lie, a lie is still a lie. He didn't find you out-front and scare you. No, you let a little money tossed your way allow you to get sucked into a crazy man's game to torture a woman he claimed to love. You turned your back on her without even giving her a chance to explain."

Corinne starts poking Keri in the chest. "You fucked up. You were told not to come around here, and yet, here you are. You're not deaf, and you're not dumb, so you're just a plain pain in the ass. Your days of sucking dick are done. Your days of a good time with any of the Hellions are done. You were told, yet you come in the bar I work at and rile up the boys I serve and just piss me off in general. So take a hike before I get you outside and give you a lesson you won't soon forget."

"I … I … I," she stutters. "You're a bitch."

Corinne laughs in her face. "Tell me something I don't already know."

Keri steps back and drops her head to look at the ground in defeat. "It was a mistake."

"Yeah, it was. Want a cookie for owning it? Nothing you can do will change it, so move on. That's what the rest of us are trying to do," Corinne adds.

I decide she has it under control, so I slide back on my stool and finish my beer.

Move on. That's what the rest of us are trying to

do. Truer words haven't been spoken in a long damn time.

I have spent weeks at a time out on the road. I have joined Rex and Tripp on transports and sometimes just hit the open road alone. Every mile between us only makes the pain feel sharper.

"Always have been on her side," Keri huffs at Corinne.

"I'll always have her back. You should look up loyalty in the dictionary. You wouldn't want your secrets shared with a stranger. Instead of thinking you were helping, maybe you should have asked Pam yourself."

Anger fills the room, and Keri puffs up her chest in defense. "Whatever. Don't turn her problems on me."

"Don't come around here, and you won't have to worry about it. You aren't wanted, and you aren't welcome, so leave before I have to have someone take the trash out or do it myself." Without another word, Corinne turns on her heel-covered foot and heads back to the bar, never missing a swish of her hips.

Loyalty. That is the Hellions.

Family. My brotherhood.

Why do I have all these people who care and still

feel like something is missing? Oh, that's because a certain purple pussy is missing. It's not just the sex, either; it's her smile, her laugh, and simply who she is; the way she feels against me, the way she soothes something deep inside of me that I didn't know was broken until she came along. Now she's gone, and I feel empty inside.

Corinne puts another longneck in front of me after she pops the top. Her blonde hair is pulled back from her face tonight, making her blue eyes stand out even more.

"She's good, you know."

"Who?" I ask, not following.

Corinne looks directly in my eyes. "Pamela, she's good. Thanks to you, Boomer, she's good."

"We all have a path to follow. She has her happily ever after. I didn't give it to her; she found her own way there."

"Boomer, you gave her the only bright moments in her darkest days. When the truth came out, you accepted and adapted. You didn't judge her. You didn't question her. You simply took care of her. She's solid now thanks to you." She taps the beer bottle. "It ain't much, but that one's on me."

"Thanks," I begin, but she shakes her head.

"None needed. You gave the only true friend I've

ever had a real life again. Take care, Boomer, and maybe take a ride sometime soon to the coast." She adds the last bit with a wink before taking off with a perfect sway of her luscious hips.

Too bad I know there isn't a passion-fruit-purple pussy under that denim skirt she's rocking. My dick only seems to want to come to life when it can be near a polka dot pussy that was molded just for me.

Maybe I should take a ride to the coast.

I tip up the drink and take a long pull. Would Pamela be open to a visit? I have called a few times and make it a point to text every day to check in. Everything between us seems closer than before.

She comes alive when she talks about the boys, about her new home, and about her life, a life she has built without me. How would she feel about me showing up? Would I remind her of what happened to Dennis?

I haven't seen her in so long. Maybe it's better if I stay away. After all, she has had this time to heal and rebuild, and I don't need to stir up bad memories.

Corinne is back in front of me, tapping a bottle opener to the glass of my longneck. "Don't think, Boomer. Go ride," she encourages. "I know our girl. She needs to reconnect, and from the looks of you over the last few months, so do you."

A simple ride to see a friend has a definite appeal.

Pamela

"**G**ood morning," I greet Amy as I make my way into work.

My time is split between cleaning the apartments for the guys, cleaning a few houses, the offices, and working with Amy in the garage reception area.

She is nice enough. We aren't close, but from what I gather, she isn't terribly close with anyone except Frisco and maybe Sass. I don't ask questions, because I know all about wanting to leave the past behind you. I just know she has panic attacks sometimes.

Whatever brought her to the Hellions was traumatic, and I'm glad she has Frisco and the club to keep her safe now.

Who would have thought I would have found safety in a motorcycle club? Who could believe that earning my place on my back would get me the chance to have a life with my boys again?

It happened. Here I am. I have my kids, my job, and I have my own place. I may not have a white picket fence, or in Hellions' form, a black picket fence, but I have a new start. My bed may be lonely at night because I long for the tall, scruffy, bearded man who gave it all to me, but that's okay since no one else measures up.

I miss Boomer. I miss him every second of every day. It seems odd that he 'claimed' me so I could be in this world and have the safety of the club, but he's not with me. The occasional call and daily text isn't enough. I don't want distance between us. I also know his life is in Catawba. Besides, my kids are good here, settled. I can't just take that away for me to take a chance on a man who may not want a family with me anymore. Now that he knows the truth, he may not think I'm so great anymore.

I worry about him, though. I worry about whether he is sleeping okay, if he's eating well, and I will be honest, I worry about who he is sleeping with.

Corinne says he hasn't taken anyone home that she has seen. She also says he seems a little sad and maybe haunted. Whether that is by what he had to do or not, I don't know.

I don't have the balls to ask.

Frisco walks in from the bays, smiling and carrying two cups of coffee. He sets one on my desk.

"Morning, Pamela."

I nod and smile. "Morning, Frisco."

He kisses the top of Amy's head innocently before setting her coffee in front of her. "Gonna be a good day."

"Sure," she whispers to him unconvincingly. "Every day is a new opportunity," she chimes the practiced sentence she tries to live by.

"I'm through the door if you need me," Frisco says, heading back out. "Have a good day, Pamela," he calls out without looking back.

Amy watches him leave, not commenting further.

The way Frisco takes care of her reminds me of Boomer. It makes me miss the nights he would take me home and simply hold me so I could sleep.

I miss the way he seemed to know exactly what I needed without me having to say anything. I miss the way he smells, the way he talks, and my goodness, the way he touches me.

It's all gone now. I need to let it go.

I have my boys, my mom, and we are safe. I need to be happy with where I am in life. I don't need more.

Keep it simple, sister. I have what I need in life: my boys safe and healthy. I can't ask for more.

The day passes by quickly as Amy and I work together to keep parts ordered and appointments scheduled for the garage. It's late afternoon when the front door chimes, and as I look up, I swear my eyes are deceiving me. I blink. His beard is still there, and a cocky smile stretches across his face.

To hell with it! Boomer is here, right in front of me. I'm not going to waste a moment questioning.

I take off from behind the counter and rush to him. He stands in front of me, and I take the biggest risk I have taken since the day I left Dennis. Reaching up, I wrap my hands around his neck and pull him down to me.

My lips brush softly against his, and he growls before opening to me. Timidly, I kiss him before his hands come around and cup my ass firmly as he takes over and devours my mouth. Rather than a simple hello, we are embraced in a loud, sloppy kiss, and I want nothing more than to keep it going.

He pulls away slowly. "Miss me?"

I smirk at him. "I won't even try to deny it."

"Good. This mean we're done playin' and you're gonna be mine?"

It's like a bowl of ice cold water is dumped on my head, and I pull away.

His grip tightens.

"Boomer," I whisper.

"Keep it simple," he says, and I stifle a laugh

since I was just reminding myself of that. "You wanna give this a chance? See what we could be?"

"Yes," I whisper, trying not to look at him.

"One step at a time."

"It's not that simple—" I start, but he puts a finger over my lips to quiet me.

"I know you've got the boys, Pami. When the time comes, we will tackle that, but first, we gotta do you and me together."

"Boomer, you live in Catawba."

"No, I live where the road takes me, and it took me here to you."

I open and close my mouth like a fish with no words coming out. *What are you saying?* I want to ask, but I can't make the sounds work.

"I haven't had much to believe in throughout my life, but I believe in us. I believe in you. I wanna see where this goes. I'm willing to come here for that chance. You just gotta decide if you're gonna give it to me."

I bite my bottom lip. This is crazy. Regardless, I nod my head because, once again, I can't get the words out.

He believes in me—he really does—and I believe in him. I believe in the man he is and the values he stands for. I believe in the things he can teach my boys just by being the man he is and setting a good example. I believe that, when he loves, it's with his whole heart and mind. I believe that Nathan 'Boomer' Vaughn is my hero, my savior, and my love. I believe, with him beside me, I can have no fears, and I can face whatever life gives me.

"Words, Pami. I want words."

"Yes, Boomer, I'm gonna give it to you," I add with a wink.

CHAPTER

TWELVE

BOOMER

Waiting for Pamela to get off work seems to take forever. Knowing she is here, I am here, and we finally seem to be on the same page, I just wanted to take her off for a ride. When five o'clock hits, I make sure to be there to take my woman away.

She smiles at me, making her way outside.

I take her by the hand and lead her to my bike. After I hand her a helmet, she steps back.

"Boomer, my car? My kids?"

"I know. I've got Ruby taking your car home.

Your mom knows you'll be home late, but before the boys go to bed."

She blinks. "Ummm, I can't."

Frustration builds inside me. I can't take the push and pull. I want her, and she wants me; why can't we simply be?

"Can't or won't?" I ask, feeling like we have been down this road enough times.

"Both," she replies honestly, and my face hardens. I'm ready to give up when she squeezes my hand. "Boomer, I don't wanna miss dinner with my boys. I had a lot of missed meals, and I don't want to miss another one if I can help it."

I'm an ass. I didn't even think. The boys—of course she wouldn't want to miss dinner with them.

She reaches up and her soft hand runs over my beard. "I'll call you after the boys are in bed. I don't want to put more on them by trying to have you in our home, but I want to see you. I know they know you as my friend from Ruby and Vida's house, but it's all been so much, and they are settling in finally." She is rambling, so I reach up and cup her chin.

"I get it." Without another word, I lean down and kiss my woman.

She opens eagerly, and our tongues dance like

long-lost lovers. When I feel her pull on me, ready for more, I pull back.

"Until tonight, Pami." I can give her this. More than that, I can give her boys the time they deserve with their mom.

She rolls up on her toes and gives me a soft kiss before pulling away. I then watch her walk to her car, and I swear she has more sway to those luscious hips than ever before. Watching her makes me hard.

My phone rings a few hours later, and I smile. For the first time in my life, I am looking forward to something. For the first time, I am really living. This isn't out of duty. This isn't out of obligation. For the first time, I don't have the urge to take off on my bike until the memories haunt me again. No, for the first time, I want to look ahead. I want to have a future with the beautiful, strong, and amazing woman who found her way into my life.

"Hey gorgeous," I answer, wanting to laugh at how much of a pussy I am over her. I don't care, though. As long as I can keep this feeling, I don't care if I have to shave my beard and turn in my man card. She can have it all.

"Hey, Boomer," she whispers.

"Boys in bed?"

"Yes. So, ummm …" I can hear the hesitation in her voice.

Trying to hide my disappointment, I give her an out. "We can take this slow, Pami. If you're tired, we can go out another night. There is no rush, honey."

"It's not that."

I blow out a relieved sigh. As much as I don't want to admit it, I need to see her. I will give her time if she really wants it, but after everything, I need to hold her. I need to inhale her sweet, cinnamon smell and squeeze her amazing curves.

"Boomer," she whispers, "I live in a doublewide."

I laugh. "I'm very aware of where you live. I don't give a shit."

"Boomer, I live in a trailer," she stresses.

I don't get why she would be embarrassed. Her home now is probably four times the size of the trailer she had in Catawba, and it's got more square footage than my cabin.

"I don't care where you live, Pami," I try to reassure her.

She laughs, and I swear it sounds better than an angel singing from Heaven.

"Boomer…" She draws out my name, and I love that sound. "I live in a not well insulated trailer with two children, and you drive a Harley Davidson motorcycle with those loud as hell pipes."

I erupt in uncontrolled laughter.

"Boomer, this isn't funny. I don't want to wake the boys."

"Oh, honey, I don't wanna wake the boys, either, but I'm sure by now they are used to the sounds of a motorcycle and won't stir."

I hear her sigh softly. "If you're sure you aren't gonna wake my boys, then what the hell are you waiting for? Get over here."

"There's my firecracker," I say, rubbing my beard. "See you in a few."

After disconnecting the call, I waste no time in getting to her house where she is waiting out front, which surprises me.

As I pull up, she comes down the steps, and my first thought is to build her a porch.

Damn, I have it bad. I can see me grilling on her front porch, drinking a beer before tossing a ball with her boys. I want this. I want this in a way I have never wanted anything before.

She stops just shy of the bike, and we sit there momentarily, watching one another. We are far from strangers, but the weight of change hangs heavily between us.

In front of me stands everything I never knew I wanted in life. In front of me is a pillar of strength and sacrifice. She would give anything to give her boys a safe future. I would give anything to give her a better future than she could ever dream.

"I ... Boomer, I—" she stutters. "I don't want to risk the boys waking and you being in the house."

I smile. My woman is the best mother to her boys, and that in itself is a bigger turn on than anything in the world.

Beauty isn't about big tits, a round ass, and blonde hair. Beauty comes from the inside and shines out. It's not about having a pussy that can milk a cock or lips that can suck the hardest. It's not about the outward appearance. Some of the most outwardly beautiful women in the world are the biggest bitches to ever be around.

No, beauty is the woman who can look beyond herself and give everything to those around her. Beauty is the sacrifice a woman makes of herself, of her body, of her mind, and of her heart to carry another being within her and breathe life.

My mom was the most beautiful woman in the world ... until I met Pamela.

The sparkle in her eyes when she thinks of her kids, the dedication she has to giving them more in life than the wrongs of their father, and the determination to see them thriving even at the greatest cost to herself, that is beauty.

I reach out and take her by the hand. I want to kiss her, but I know in this moment, if I do, I won't stop. She's a mom, and the last thing I will do is fuck her on the front lawn, even if the caveman inside me wants to.

"Ride with me?" I ask with a smile.

She looks deep into my eyes. There are no secrets between us now. I know the path she has walked has been far from easy. I know the life she has led has made her a little jaded. All of that is over now. I will give everything until my dying breath to make sure she never feels pain like she has endured ever again.

She smiles back at me. "Anytime, Boomer."

Without hesitation, she takes the helmet from behind me and puts it on before climbing behind me. Her thighs are snug around me, her chest pressed against my back as her arms wrap around me. I have no sissy bar, so she leans into me, settling in.

I breathe deep.

Comfort. Trust. Faith.

Love.

I look to the sky above where the stars shine brightly tonight, and I can only hope my mom is smiling down at the man she sees today. I will give everything I have to make Pami's life better than it's ever been before.

I tip my pointer finger to the sky in acknowledgement to the woman who gave me life before I twist the throttle and pull away with the woman who gives me new life today firmly behind me.

Pamela

The wind circles around us, but all I feel is him in front of me.

Is this real? Boomer is really here for me?

I look up to the stars in the sky. Is this my second chance at life, at love?

Having this time to rebuild my life, I have learned to appreciate all that Boomer has given not only to me, but to my boys and my mom. No longer does my mom have to lie awake at night, wondering if I am going to call her from a hospital, telling her Dennis has taken more than the life of our unborn daughter. No longer does she have to worry something will happen to me and she won't know. No longer does she have to carry the burden of raising my boys on her own. Boomer and the Hellions have taken us into the fold and given us all everything I never thought it was possible to have.

I didn't think it could get any better … until he showed up today. Having Boomer here, kissing me, touching me, taking me for a ride, it is so much more than I ever imagined. Having a real chance to have something with him, icing on the cake of my new life.

I squeeze tighter as the pavement passes under us. We reach the high-rise bridge that takes us over to the beach, and I feel the wind whip around us, and the salt in the air fills my lungs.

He makes the right at the light and takes us down the winding road to 'The Point.' Parking, we get off the Harley then make our way beyond the gate to the sandy beach.

The waves crashing on the shore are a soothing reminder that my life is good now. Hit after Hit, my life was pummeled, but there is no more crashing around me.

I reach out and take Boomer's hand. He has given me the freedom to be here in this moment without hesitation.

I inhale deeply, the smell of the beach invading and comforting me as we walk to the dunes where Boomer sits against one then places me facing the ocean with my back to his chest as I sit between his legs.

"Pami …" He starts massaging my shoulders. "I missed you."

I moan as I relax into him. "I missed you," I whisper back.

We both stare out and watch the waves come to shore as he continues to rub the tension from my shoulders and neck.

He kisses my temple. "Future looks good."

I turn to face him. Cupping his chin, I run my thumb over his beard. "You are beautiful."

He laughs. "I'm far from beautiful."

"You're amazing," I whisper, running my thumb over his bottom lip. "Not many men would find me worth—"

"Shhh," he interrupts. "Pamela, do not finish that sentence. You're worth it, your boys are worth it, and the life we are gonna have together is worth everything and more." He kisses my forehead. "Never had something to live for until you and now your boys. My drive, honey, my everything is you and what we can build together. The future is looking bright."

He is so certain, and I can't help feeling confident in the future we can build together.

Moving in, I brush my lips to his. Twisting, I then

crawl up him, pushing him back against the side of the dune as I go. I use my teeth to pull at his bottom lip, the feeling of his beard tickling my chin as he growls and leans into me while his hands come around to squeeze my ass, pushing my body into his.

I feel alive. In his arms, I feel safe, cherished, and I feel like a woman who is wanted.

My nipples harden behind the cotton material of my cheap bra. I push the insecurity away as his mouth opens and his tongue meets my lips, seeking entrance I gladly give. Our tongues mingle and explore as I slide up his body, resting my hips over his, feeling him harden against my belly, which makes me want more.

He pulls back and breathes deeply. "Pami, it's not about this. You don't have to—"

I cut him off with a kiss.

Once we are both breathless, I pull away to look in his eyes so he can see there are no more secrets between us. "I want this, I want you, and I want a future between us."

He slides his hands up my back then pulls my head down to his lips as he kisses me with passion, lust, and desire.

Moving, I straddle him then push his cut off, smiling as he leans up and pulls his shirt off. I do the same with my shirt. Before I can remove my bra, though, his hands pull my breasts from their cups, and he tweaks one nipple as he takes the other in his mouth and sucks. I arch back, giving him better access. My core aches for attention as I grind my jeans over him.

"Boomer," I cry out as his hands move to unbutton and unzip my pants. "More. I need more."

He slides them over my ass, letting them tighten around my thighs as he dips his hand inside my panties and rubs my pussy, circling my clit before he pulls his hand away.

I groan at the loss of contact.

"Stand up. Pants off. Panties, too," he commands as he pushes back to unbutton and unzip his jeans, freeing his cock.

I lick my lips in desire as I do as told. Then he takes my hands and guides me to stand over him. Grabbing my ass, he pulls my pussy to his face. His tongue separates my lips, and then, using his thumbs, he massages inside my thighs at the edge of my pussy, relaxing my muscles more as he licks, nips, and then sucks on my clit. My legs tremble as my orgasm builds.

"Let go, beautiful," Boomer says against my pussy before grazing his teeth over my outer lips.

He uses his fingers to expose me then slides his thumb inside. He draws lazy circles at the very edge of my entrance as he blows against my clit.

Anticipation builds before his mouth is hot against me, his tongue flicking against my clit and sending me soaring.

When I can't hold myself up, he moves me to straddle him.

"We can stop," he whispers.

"Boomer, I want this. I want you." I take his cock in my hand and stroke twice, feeling the pre-come at the tip. Then I bite my bottom lip as I guide him inside me.

Wrapping my hands around his neck, I slide up and down his length as he looks deep into my eyes. Unsaid emotions are passing between us. No words are needed; we simply are. Boomer and me.

He cups my ass as he lets me take my time and savor the sensation of him connected to me and filling me. I grind down until I can't go any farther and roll my hips, pushing my breasts against him. My bra pushes them higher, and Boomer obliges by taking one in his mouth and sucking hard while his hands pull my ass cheeks apart, making my pussy clinch tighter around his cock.

"Boomer," I cry out as the sensations overwhelm me.

"Give it to me, beautiful. Give it all to me," he whispers, looking into my eyes.

"It's all yours, Boomer."

"Love you, Pami. Took a long time to figure shit out, but real deal, simple as that, I love you."

Tears fill my eyes. "I never thought I would feel this way, never thought I would have it so good." I slide up then down again, stilling myself to look into the dark brown eyes that have been my safe haven for so long now. "I love you, Boomer."

At my words, he takes over and begins to guide my hips, never taking his eyes from mine. As he picks up the pace, my walls tighten and my release builds. The heat of his explosion inside me sends me over, and I come around him, moaning in satisfaction.

He holds my hips down as he finishes spilling his seed inside of me, and I drop my head to his shoulder as I try to bring myself back down.

He pushes my hair back off my shoulders. "Beautiful. You are simply beautiful."

I smile against him. I could get used to this. I want to get used to this. I want more of this, and I never want it to end.

EPILOGUE

Epilogue

One Year Later ...

Pamela

The knock at the door makes me smile. No longer do I have fear or tension of who will come over. No, nowadays, my boys and I have a normal life.

"Hey, RJ," I greet Vida's son.

"Can Wes and Colt come play? Papa will be home soon, and I can only play till dinner time." The boy looks up at me just as my boys come running up the hallway to see their friend.

"Sure thing," I reply, moving swiftly out of the way to watch the boys dash into the front yard.

It's not long before I hear the sounds of a Harley coming up the driveway. Moving to the door so I can call the boys inside and send RJ home, I am surprised to see Boomer's truck behind my car along with Ruby's bike. Vida is walking over from her house, I assume to gather up her son.

I step off my front steps and into the yard just in time to watch Boomer unfold from his truck.

"Wesson, Colt, come over here and help an old man out."

"Boomer, you're not old. Memaw is old. You're nowhere near that," Wesson says as he jogs over and quickly gives Boomer a hug. Colt follows not far behind, and my heart swells with pride and love as I look at the bond my boys have found with the man who has given us everything.

Boomer looks up, meeting my gaze. He simply nods to me.

That's how it is with us. I don't need poetic accolades, nor do I need him to rush over and sweep me off my feet. The way he gives my whole life, the very pieces of my world, attention is what makes us work.

Boomer is everything I ever needed and more, and I didn't even know it. Simply us and it simply works.

"Hey, Pami," Vida greets, meeting up with me as we both make our way across my yard and to our men who are focused on getting something out of the back of Boomer's truck.

"Score for Wes and Colt!" RJ screams as I see Ruby and Boomer unloading two bicycles. "You got the ones like Papa made for us! Ride like a Hellion."

"Really? Are these for us, Boomer?" Colt asks.

"I call red," Wesson makes his claim as Boomer smiles down at my—no, our boys.

We had that talk, the conversation I was sure would send him away. Telling Boomer I had my tubes tied and that I had no desire to have it undone was a tough conversation. However, it was necessary. I didn't want to build something with him and have there be any secrets between us.

Nathan 'Boomer' Vaughn is an amazing man, full of love and compassion. He would be the best father to a child of his own. For me, though, I don't want to do that to my boys. I don't want to take anything away from the time I have with them. I feel like I owe them so many memories that I can't imagine bringing another baby into our family. If that was a deal breaker for Boomer, we needed to address it before I brought him into my boys' lives. Once again, the man proved just what a perfect man he is for us.

"Pami," he told me, "I didn't have a life before you. I had a mom who did it all on her own. She gave me good, honey. I'm gonna give you and your boys good. I'm a simple man, and I got all I need in you and your family, baby."

Just like that, we moved on together, and now here he is with bikes for my boys. Not just any bikes, either, custom designed, Hellions' bicycles.

"Gotta start 'em young," Ruby says, smiling at me.

I laugh as I watch Wesson taking in the bike that has been outfitted with a fabricated gas tank, saddle-bags, and even rearview mirrors.

"Safety," Boomer says, winking at me as he pulls a matching black bike down for Colt, while Ruby helps the boys put on their helmets.

Wesson immediately hops on the bike and takes off with only a mild wobble. That's my youngest, though; he has always faced things head-on and taken off. He's fearless where Colton thinks everything through.

Colt looks at me as I wrap my arm around Boomer's waist. Then he looks at Boomer holding the bike by the handlebars, but Colt doesn't move.

Ruby makes his way to Vida and wraps her in his arms, planting a firm kiss to her lips like he does every time he gets close to her. RJ runs off to his house to get his own bike as his sisters play in their front yard.

Colt moves over to Boomer, looking at me then to the man beside me.

Boomer squats down to get eye-level with my son. "You all right, Colt?" he asks, and my son leans over to whisper in his ear.

I can't hear what he says, only see the fear in his eyes.

Boomer nods his head and stands. Taking my son's bike with his right hand, he extends his left for Colt. My boy releases the bike, and hand in hand, Boomer guides them out to our quiet street.

I watch with tears filling my eyes as Boomer shows my baby boy the brakes, the mirrors, the pedals, the chain, and every piece to the bike.

I move closer to hear Boomer say, "We can get you some training wheels if you want, or we can try it out and see how you do. I'll hold on to your seat from the back."

"Don't let go," Colt pleads.

"Never," Boomer reassures him. "That's how it is

in the Hellions, Colt. We never let go, and we always have your back."

If that isn't the truth of the motorcycle club I have found my way into, I don't know what is.

I look to my little boy who smiles proudly at the man who has captured my heart.

"Then what are we waitin' for? Let's ride, Boomer."

I think to myself, *let's ride for life, Boomer. Simple as that.*

BOOMER

Sometimes, things have to go slowly. Pamela and I are a testament to this.

After being apart for so long, I didn't want to encroach on her reestablishing her place with her boys. On the other hand, I didn't want to be almost six hours from the woman I have fallen in love with. Having no real roots in Catawba other than the Hellions and Shooter, making the move to Haywood's Landing wasn't hard.

I sold my cabin and land, turning a decent profit.

Making the move, I was able to buy a few acres not far from the compound and build a place big enough for Pami, her boys, and her mom to live. It may seem crazy that I left my life behind to keep her from having to uproot her kids again, but my life is where she is.

Now I only have one last piece of my past I need to put to rest so I can move on with my future.

As I pull into the driveway, his gray Ford truck sits in the driveway just like it did years ago. I look up to the blue sky above and hope he is watching. I hope he can see that, even though I felt like it should have been me, I have somehow made it through.

Climbing off my bike, I head to the front door and ring the bell. It's not long before Melonie opens the door.

"Boomer," she greets in surprise.

"Melonie." I lean in and hug her.

She steps back, and I enter the home of my friend's widow and feel the weight lifted off as I see the pictures lining the walls of her son.

"Boomer, what brings you here?"

"Wanted to check on you."

She reaches out and squeezes my hand. "We're good, Boomer. You can let go."

I squeeze her hand back. "Never, Melonie."

Tears fill her eyes. "We're good. I want you to know that."

"If you ever need anything—"

"I'll call. You've gotta let go, Boomer. Life goes on. Skid died doing what he loved to do. He left this world with honor and integrity. Don't let that be wasted. You've gotta live life, Boomer."

Seeing the sincerity in her eyes and knowing she genuinely cares, I am proud to stand before her as the man I am today.

I pull her into me and hug her tightly.

"Boomer, talk to me. Something has changed." She's never been one to hold back.

"There have been a lot of years I wished I could turn back the hands of time. I wanted to give him back to you."

She pulls away, and I see the tears fall down her face. "I have him with me, Boomer. No one can take him from me not the Army or the enemy. He's in my heart; he's in my child; he's forever in my world."

"I never felt like I had a purpose. Always was a drifter. I did what I had to do, but I existed. Then we lost Skid, and I couldn't move on like it didn't happen. I rode wherever the road would take me for a lot of years, Mel. It took a long time, but it brought me to a place, and I found someone."

Her eyes light up and a smile creeps across her lips. "I've been worried about you."

"I would still trade places with him; you know that, right? No matter what, if I could, I would trade places with him so you wouldn't have to bear the pain." It's the truth. As happy as I am, I would give it all away to give my brother back his life.

"With pain comes healing, Boomer. I value the time I had with him, the gifts of the memories we made. You know, not everyone finds a love like I had. Not everyone gets to marry their very best friend. Not everyone gets to know a man who will stand up to the very end for the values he believes in. My husband did that. My husband gave his last breath serving someone other than himself. Boomer, you've gotta find that love. You've gotta give some woman that kind of man."

She is okay. I needed this. I needed the closure.

I give her another hug and pull away. "I have that."

"Then hold on tight and make every moment count. Don't take one second for granted. Keep it simple. You love through the good times and the bad. You love through the close times and beyond any distance. Boomer, no matter what happens, you simply love each other through it."

———

"**B**oomer, I don't think we're supposed to be here."

I laugh. "Where is your rebellious side, Pami?"

"At home with my kids," she replies dryly. "Seriously, someone bought this place months ago. I don't think they would appreciate us being here." She doesn't know I sold my cabin. She doesn't know I bought the field with the old farm house and had it remodeled.

I have been living in one of the duplexes Roundman has on the compound while Pamela and I have been getting to know each other better and introducing me into her sons' lives. Over time, I have had enough sleepovers that I live in her doublewide with them more than at the compound, even though we haven't made living together official.

I want more than that, though. I want it all, and I want it all officially.

Reaching over the cab of truck, I squeeze her hand. "Trust me." I then climb out and round the hood, making my way to open her door.

"I should've known you were up to trouble today when we didn't take the bike out, and we don't have the boys."

"I love the sound of that."

She reaches up and checks my forehead. "No fever. Are you crazy today? The sound of what?"

"We and boys in the same sentence."

She laughs, and my heart beats faster.

"Boomer, the boys love you." Tears fill her eyes. "You-you …" She inhales deeply. "Boomer, you're everything they've never had, everything we've never had."

Leaning in, I brush my lips over hers.

As much as I want to get lost in the moment with her, I can't. No, I have so much more to take care of first.

"I love them, Pami."

She nods, knowing it's the damn truth. Then she takes my hand and hops out of the truck. I turn her to face the two-story farm house with the large wrap-around porch.

"One day," she sighs.

"Remember when the sign went up and you said how you saw the potential in this place being restored?"

She nods her head.

"You said you would keep it white with black shutters; only, you would make the front columns black instead of white."

She takes in the house and the black columns in front of her.

"I believe it was a red door you always wanted."

She looks to the red front door and nods her head.

I step away and go to the back of the truck to reach under the tarp. Her eyes go wide as she looks at what I removed.

"Well, I had to buy it in white, but Sass and Vida helped make it black for you, honey. I remember you saying once how you liked the idea of a black picket fence, too."

She shakes her head as tears fall down her face. "No."

I nod. "Yeah," I say, moving the fence panel to the edge and laying it on the ground in front of us.

"Boomer, no."

The shock on her face has me on edge.

"That's not exactly the reaction I was going for, honey."

She covers her face. "You-you-you did all this?"

"Well, I was thinking more along the lines of we and the future."

"Boomer …"

"Pami, it's been a long, turbulent ride to get to this place. Not one damn thing has been easy except thinking of my future with you and the boys. Giving you everything you never had, carrying your burdens with you side by side, that takes away the pain of the past."

I pull the black, velvet box from my pocket and drop to one knee in front of her. "Don't over-think, don't overdo, just listen … I want to give you the simple life. I want to be the man you turn to at night and smile at in the morning. I want to be the man your boys look up to, and I want to teach them to appreciate good when it's right in front of them. I want us to grow old together in this house that was a mess until, together, we made it beautiful.

"I was a mess before you came into my life. I was drowning in regret, and you gave me a reason to be again. Everything complicated became simple with you, because of you. I love you, Pamela, and I want to ride for life with you on my bike and by my side.

"I am not a man of material things; I am a man with a heart that beats for you and your children. I am a man who is on his knee, giving you a promise of a lifetime together—a lifetime where you will be safe; you will be cherished; you will be loved. I am a man who promises to love your children as my own and teach them what it is to be a man of honor. I am a man who promises to walk hand in hand with you through the good times and the bad.

"Ride with me, Pami? Give me the black picket fence? The simple life. Marry me, Pami?"

"Never in my life did I believe fairytales or a happily ever after would happen again after … everything." She pauses, thinking. "Boomer, never did I have hope in my hopeless situation. Nothing about us is simple, but everything between us simply is. I would be proud to be Mrs. Nathan 'Boomer' Vaughn. I want nothing more than the simple ride with you for the rest of our days."

~The End~

Until the next ride.

ABOUT THE AUTHOR

USA Today and *Wall Street Journal* bestselling author Chelsea Camaron is a small-town Carolina girl with a big imagination. She's a wife and mom, chasing her dreams. She writes contemporary romance, erotic suspense, and psychological thrillers. She loves to write about blue-collar men who have real problems with a fictional twist. From mechanics to bikers to oil riggers to smokejumpers, bar owners, and beyond she loves a strong hero who works hard and plays harder.

Chelsea can be found on social media at:

Facebook www.facebook.com/authorchelseacamaron
Twitter @chelseacamaron
Email chelseacamaron@gmail.com

ALSO BY CHELSEA CAMARON

Love and Repair Series:

Crash and Burn

Restore My Heart

Salvaged

Full Throttle

Beyond Repair

Stalled

Box Set Available

Hellions Ride Series:

One Ride

Forever Ride

Merciless Ride

Eternal Ride

Innocent Ride

Simple Ride

Heated Ride

Ride with Me (Hellions MC and Ravage MC Duel with

Ryan Michele)

Originals Ride

Final Ride

Hellions Ride On Series:

Hellions Ride On Prequel

Born to It

Bastard in It

Bleed for It

Breathe for It

Bold from It

Broken by It

Brazen being It

Better as It

Blue Collar Bad Boys Series:

Maverick

Heath

Lance

Wendol

Reese

Devil's Due MC Series:

Serving My Soldier

Crossover

In The Red

Below The Line

Close The Tab

Day of Reckoning

Paid in Full

Bottom Line

Almanza Crime Family Duet

Cartel Bitch

Cartel Queen

Romantic Thriller Series:

Stay

Seeking Solace: Angelina's Restoration

Reclaiming Me: Fallyn's Revenge

Bad Boys of the Road Series:

Mother Trucker

Panty Snatcher

Azzhat

Santa, Bring Me a Biker!

Santa, Bring Me a Baby!

Stand Alone Reads:

Romance – Moments in Time Anthology

Shenanigans (Currently found in the Beer Goggles
Anthology

She is …

The following series are co-written

The Fire Inside Series:

(co-written by Theresa Marguerite Hewitt)

Kale

Regulators MC Series:

(co-written by Jessie Lane)

Ice

Hammer

Coal

Summer of Sin Series:

(co-written with Ripp Baker, Daryl Banner, Angelica

Chase, MJ Fields, MX King)

Original Sin

Caldwell Brothers Series:

(co-written by USA Today Bestselling Author MJ Fields)

Hendrix

Morrison

Jagger

Stand Alone Romance:

(co-written with USA Today Bestselling Author MJ Fields)

Visibly Broken

Use Me

Ruthless Rebels MC Series:

(co-written with Ryan Michele)

Shamed

Scorned

Scarred

Schooled

Box Set Available

Power Chain Series:

(co-written with Ryan Michele)

HEATED RIDE

Hellions Ride Series Book 7

The Hellions motorcycle club is a commitment for life, one Ruben 'Ruby' Castillo believes in.

His wife Jenna 'Vida' Natera de Castillo has given her life to being his ol' lady and the mother to their three children. She takes her commitment to her man seriously.

People change, and over time, passion can fizzle. Life for Jenna falls apart the day Ruby no longer says I do.

Keeping the fires burning in a marriage is hard. Will the chaos of the club bring them back together, or is it what pulls them further apart? Will these two find the flame again? Will their love find a new spark on their heated ride through life?

RUBY

Excerpt

Ruby

Eat. Sleep. Shit. Shower. Work.

Ride.

Wash, rinse, and repeat. That's my life.

When did everything become the same?

I walk into my home, and there is a part of me that wants to turn and walk right back out the door. Behind the stove—making an amazing dinner, I'm sure—is my wife, my life, my "Vida." Her long, dark hair is braided behind her back as she studies the pan in front of her, humming to herself. Standing in the doorway, I study her. I study our life.

There are worry lines on her forehead. I remember

when her face was flawless. My best friend's little sister, my amigo from way back, somehow worked her way into my blackened heart. She filled every void I ever had as a boy and helped me grow into a man.

Ride or die, she's been by my side.

I step into the living room where I immediately step on a car little RJ left on the floor, and I can't stop the irritation that builds inside me.

When did my life go from dodging bullets to dodging fucking toys?

Are we too comfortable? Is this all we have left? Getting wrinkles and raising babies?

Vida looks up at me and smiles the same smile she has smiled for the last fifteen years, the smile that still brings my cock to attention.

I study her. She looks tired. No makeup covers her face. She's in sweats and an old T-shirt I could swear each of our babies has puked on more than once. She sees me, and still, she smiles.

Her body has grown. She has changed. With the swell of each pregnancy, she grew and glowed. After each baby, she got curvier. She isn't large, but she is no longer the tiny, no hips, tits, or ass she once was. No, my woman, my wife, my life has curves.

Smugly, I think, *Yeah, I gave her those curves.*

Every time I planted my seed so deep, I gave her curves.

I make my way to the stove where I wrap my arms around her waist and pull her to me. I kiss her, and she opens readily for my tongue to greet hers.

Now, this is the life.

Her arms wrap around my neck as she kisses me back.

I'm lost in my woman's arms, in her mouth, and in her touch. No matter what goes on, I can get lost in Vida.

She pulls away, still smiling. "I gotta cook, Ruby."

"Turn it off, and I'll turn you on."

She pats my chest before turning back to her meal preparation. "Maybe later. The babies need to eat."

Babies, my ass. Our kids are now nine, seven, and five. They can wait thirty minutes for me to take my wife to the bedroom and have my way with her.

I move behind her and pull her braid to the right, exposing the left side of her neck to me. I lean in and suck … hard.

She pushes her ass into me to get space. "I said not now, Ruby. Geez, I gotta feed the babies and then move the laundry. I've been at work all day, and now I have a house to manage," she snaps.

I'm a motherfucking Hellion. Pussy is thrown at me constantly, but not the pussy I want. When did this happen? Where did the woman I married go? Where is the girl who couldn't get enough of my cock when we were mere teens?

When did everything change?

RAVAGE ME BY RYAN MICHELE EXCERPT

Here's an excerpt from
Ravage Me (Ravage MC#1)
©Ryan Michele 2013

PROLOGUE

This was the life I was born into, and bloodshed somehow always played a prominent part in it. Today, everything was coming to a combustible head. With the gun being held at my temple, all I could think about was *him*… getting him out of here alive. The bitch had put so much time and energy into coming after me, I knew it was coming. Now she had the most precious thing in my life. I never knew how empty my life was or how love could be so deep that it cuts you like a knife. I would do anything to get him out of here alive. The gunshots began, and my eyes locked with his. I prayed for survival.

HARLOW

2 years… 1 month… 5 days…

I had been living the perpetual monotony of my life for exactly two years, one month, and five days. It's like my life was the epitome of Groundhog's Day, repeating over and over again, eating away at my soul.

I hated white. I couldn't stand the fucking color. Everywhere I looked was the same cold, damp, sterility trying to suffocate me, forcing me to give up —to give in. But that wasn't gonna happen.

For seven hundred and sixty five days of my life, I've stared at the solid block walls and cold prison bars, only to be let outside for an hour a day. I knew it was for my own safety, but I missed lying outside in the sun, feeling it melt my skin, and wash everything away. In here, there was no relaxation… ever.

I'm not gonna bitch. I've been extremely lucky, and I damn well knew it. Without my Pops' connections to guards and powerful people on the outside, life in this place could have been a hell of a lot worse. Having my own room has proved to be the best gig because, in there, those bitches couldn't get to me. They wanted me. I knew it. They all knew who I was and what I represented. Payback hits on me would give them status in their families and I wasn't willing to give anyone that.

Am I hiding? Hell no. I'd be more than happy to take these bitches on, but not here. The shit these women snuck in when no one was looking was deadly, and my goal was to do my time and get out alive. I knew what these bitches were capable of, and they knew my capabilities, too.

I've had my own incidents in here. They were all club related, and getting help from inside made them happen smoothly. It was help that I had to pay for, but I did what needed to be done and didn't regret a damn thing. I did it for my family.

I may have a pussy, but I ain't one. I've got bigger balls than most guys out there. Even though I'll never be a member of the club, because it's not possible, I always hold my head up high. I learned at a very young age that bitches didn't ever get patched in, and I accepted that, but I'd be damned if I acted like some pussy motorcycle club princess.

Growing up with the Ravage MC's hasn't been easy. The life, the world, was different than civilian life and I learned from the best. Ever since I was a baby, my life was the club. Pops has been a patched member since before I was born, and Ma's always been by his side. Even though I was shielded as much as possible, I've seen my share of death, guns, drugs, sex, and blood in my twenty-five years than most people could tolerate. This was my normal. This was my reality. I accepted that a long time ago.

I missed my life, and I've always known my place in it. Being the Vice President's daughter hasn't given me any idealizations that I'm anything more than exactly that. I never get special privileges because, the bottom line, I'm not, nor will I ever be, a patched member. I've earned the respect I received from the brothers by learning what they have taken the time to teach me. I thrived on that and couldn't wait to get it back.

I was ready to escape this hell-hole and finally go back to my family. Back to a life that was taken away from me for two years, back to right some wrongs. I couldn't fucking wait.

W alking down the long corridor, the sunlight cascaded through the small rectangular window. I began blinking my eyes, getting ready for the adjustment when the door opened. I've never liked surprises—they get you killed, quickly. I hoped my outside instincts kicked back in after all this time. It's the one thing I've been afraid of losing. I've learned to keep myself sharp inside to stay alive, but being free was a different kind of survival.

"Here." The cold tone of the guard, something I'll never miss, ordered me forward. Some of these assholes were utterly worthless individuals who preyed on women daily. Luckily, I've only had two encounters with said assholes. When I broke the first one's nose, he decided I wasn't worth the hassle. It got me locked in solitary for a few days and a few bruises, but I actually liked it there. I was left alone. I thought about doing it again, maybe get an extended stay, but my mind always reverted to survival, and getting the hell out of here the easiest way possible.

The other, I've tried to block out of my head. As soon as my feet step outside this door, I would forget what he did, and not a single soul would ever know.

I watched as the guard's hand extended from his body, holding a clear plastic bag. Reaching for it, not much was inside. The clothes I was wearing when I got in this hell-hole were ripped when I didn't move as quickly as the officer said, so only a few items remained. Inside the bag was the cross necklace I wore that night, my ID, and a few dollars in cash. The cash actually surprised me; I was sure that would have disappeared by now with all the crooked-ass people inside.

"Gavelson!" I didn't want to turn toward the voice, not with the exit so close. But I knew they still owned me until I stepped out that door. Until then, I needed to mind myself.

"Yes, sir," I said, slowly turning around to see the warden coming closer. His stocky build with his over-sized stomach hanging over his uniform pants was nothing to get wet about, but he proved a good ally while I was inside. Warden Dunn was on Pops's payroll and set me up with my nice surroundings. He even passed certain things along from Pops during my stay. So I respected him as much as a person could while locked up. Did I trust him? No. The moment you trusted someone in here, you ended up dead.

Looking directly into my eyes, I saw a splash of concern come across his as he tilted his head slowly to the side. His voice reminded me of a whiny teenager, even though he was nowhere near his teenage years. His voice sounded raspy as if he was going through *the change* all over again. "You don't come back here, girl."

"I'll do my best," I answered, immediately knowing there were never any guarantees in this life, and your word was your only bond. If you didn't have that, you had nothing. I wasn't about to make him a promise; I didn't know for sure I could keep. I would definitely do my damnedest never to step foot in here again, though.

"Take care, Princess," the warden whispered while patting my shoulder gently. My blood boiled when I turned to walk back towards the door. I've spent my entire life trying to prove to everyone that I was no damn princess, but that name kept following me around like shit stuck to my shoe. Many women in my world would love that title. To me, though, it represented weakness. I couldn't afford to be associated with weakness.

When the guard opened the door, the bright light blinded me. I blinked quickly to get my bearings. Shielding my eyes with my hand, I looked around until I spotted the familiar, red '56 Chevy with the white flames painted on the front hood. More importantly, I spotted the woman standing next to it, Casey.

"Well don't you have a shit-eating grin on your face." Casey's smile was one of the most beautiful I'd ever seen on a woman. With her golden locks and flawless figure, she could get anyone she wanted, whenever she wanted, but damn if she used it to her advantage. Casey and I have been friends since we were kids, growing up at the club, right alongside each other. Her dad, Bam, was a patched member, who died a few years ago.

We've experienced everything together. She was my ultimate partner in crime and damn did I miss her. Grabbing her face between my hands, I stared into her emerald eyes before kissing her full on the lips. They tasted like cherries, reminding me of the little things that I've missed. Then I moved and kissed her once on each cheek.

"Well, hello to you too, girl." She laughed at my

gesture and wrapped her arms tightly around me squeezing the ever-loving shit out of me.

Stepping back, "I just missed ya, babe. Get me the hell out of here." Throwing open the car door; I hopped into the beautiful piece of machinery. The sleek car was the ultimate ride, a classic. In our world, it was called a cage, since anything that isn't a motor-cycle was considered just that.

Casey's father helped her fix it up at the shop, spending hours and hours perfecting it. He taught her everything that she'd ever have to know about fixing cars and bikes. When her father died, this car was the only connection to him she had. She treasured it more than anything on this planet and took care of it like she was loving her child.

Casey worked at the shop, Banner Automotive, attached to the Club. She may be beautiful and girly, but give her a wrench and an engine, and she was all over it. Not to mention, I've been told the guys really like the tight-ass jeans she wears. Men are so damn predictable.

"Sure thing, you ready to get that mop tamed?" Casey's eyes travelled over my ugly, stringy, brassy brown hair. I knew I looked like shit, which was why it was the first order of business.

"Absolutely."

After three hours in the chair, chatting it up with Cam while she worked her magic on my hair, I felt like a new woman. My dark brown hair was back in place with the bright streaks of red, just like I liked it. Instead of stringy, it was soft and silky. The natural wave was always a plus. Keeping it long in jail was a feat I never wanted to repeat. Just because my Pops had guys on the payroll, didn't mean that things were handed to me. I had to earn it, and damn it if I didn't. Not that I ever wanted to relive any of that again.

The drive to our place was quick, and I couldn't wait to get the hell out of these prison clothes. I needed to get the stench of that place off of me. Wrapping my hair up, I jumped in the shower letting the water wash away the two previous years of hell. After turning into a prune, I exited getting myself together quickly. I found my favorite pair of jeans with the thousands of holes in all the right places and my tight, black Harley t-shirt. After a bit of makeup, I was ready to go see my family.

Walking into the living room, Casey was flopped on the couch with the remote in her hand, thumbing endlessly through the channels. "Where is she?" I asked, wanting my girl back.

"Come on." Casey got up and headed towards her room, with me following closely behind. She dug through her closet, pulling out a locked box. Casey walked the box over to her dresser and placed it softly on the top. She rummaged through her top drawer, pulling out keys and unlocking the box.

Sitting inside was my girl. 9mm's of power that fit the palm of my hand perfectly. I learned how to shoot with this gun. My dad gave it to me when I was fourteen, and I never leave home without her.

Feeling the weight in my hand, I thumbed the beautiful piece of metal, feeling happy and at peace. I always felt protected when this was with me. It's one of the things that kept me alive for this long. Not only am I fast, but I am a great shot. Two years was a long time with no practice, though. I needed to get to the firing range and shoot off some rounds.

Checking my gun, I made sure the bullet chamber was fully loaded. I locked the safety, gave it a soft kiss, and placed it underneath my shirt in a small holster on my back.

Casey wrapped her arms around me, hugging me tightly, which I returned. "I'm so glad you're back," she whispered softly in my ear.

"Me too. Let's go see the boys."

I pulled away staring into her eyes. She was the one person that I knew would always have my back no matter what. "Let's go." She smiled, pulling my arm through the door.

Driving through the streets of Sumner, Georgia, everything seemed exactly the same as before I left. The same shops and banks lined the center of town with people walking through the streets without a care in the world. They were free, just like I was, and how I was going to stay.

Good people lived here. They were honest people; well, for the most part. When the outsiders came in, that's when we had problems.

Unfortunately, I've been kept in the dark about most of what was going on with the club. When Ma came to visit, she never discussed the brothers, and I never asked. People were always listening to us, and neither of us could risk it. I didn't know the good or the bad of what was going on, and I felt quite lost. Ma would only say that my family loved me. I knew that.

What I didn't know was what I would walk into once I got to the shop and the club. It was a bit unnerving, but I couldn't let that show. I'd never show any weakness… ever.

Pulling up to the locked gates with barbed wire lacing the top, the smile that was plastered on my face was irreversible. I was finally home.

A man I'd never seen before, wearing a Prospect

rag, came to the side of the window. "Hey, Casey. You working today?"

Smiling widely at him, she reached over and grabbed my hand, squeezing it tightly. He was pretty hot for a newbie Prospect. His dark hair hung low covering his ears, but not quite down to his shoulders. His brown eyes were the color of chocolate, matching the smoothness of his voice. His nose looked like it had taken one too many beatings over the years and hadn't been set quite right. He had a very hot, dangerous persona.

Squeezing Casey's hand back to let her know I understood his hotness, she finally spoke. "Hey, Tug. I brought Harlow home."

Tug looked me up and down, eyeing me. "Get a good look there, Bud," I said with my signature smirk that I knew would make him putty in my hands.

"Sure thing, Sweetheart. So you're the famous Princess, huh?" Rolling my eyes, I turned to face the windshield already done with the conversation. Spending your entire life trying to prove something wrong was exhausting, and I knew everyone here would be calling me that word.

"Let's go," I said, snapping my fingers in front of me, pointing to the gate.

"Your Pops is real excited to see ya, but they're in

church. They'll be out soon." Tug turned to the gate, throwing the switch to unlock the steel doors. They began to move, opening wide.

When the gates spread, I took in the view. To the left was the shop, Banner Automotive. This was one of the businesses the Ravage MC owned that did really well, not to mention they all needed some place to work on their bikes. My mom worked there doing the books and handling all the clients that came in and out through another entrance, opposite of where all the guys come in. She'd been doing it since I was a kid. I spent a lot of time in that office with Ma. My eyes scanned to the members and Prospect only parking to the right. One parking spot after the other and I could name the owners of almost every one of them. That's how I knew there were five new guys, either patched in or Prospects.

Casey parked the car in front of the shop doors and killed the engine. Walking in, it actually felt eerie. I didn't recognize anyone, but they all said hi to Casey. I should have expected a new crew of workers; they rotated quite often. Club business was kept separate from the shop. I could feel their eyes boring into me, but I kept my eyes trained on the back door. I wanted to see my man.

"Ma'am, you can't go back there!" one of the guys called out.

"The hell I can't." I began marching towards the door, knowing that my own personal heaven was on the other side. I had to see him. I had to feel him between my thighs. One of the guys grabbed my arm, turning me to look at him square in the eyes. He was pretty cute, in that rough-mechanic-having-my-hands-dirty-all-the-time, kind of a way. His blonde hair was cut very short, and his green eyes were the color of leaves.

If I wasn't so pissed that he actually put his hands on me, I might have been really attracted to him, but right now, I was livid.

"I said you're not going back there. Why the hell did you bring this slut around?" he accused Casey. This guy went from cute to an ass in about two seconds. Before Casey could say anything, I wrenched my arm out of his grasp and swung, my fist crashing into the guy's nose, squirting blood everywhere. "You bitch! Call Diamond!" he barked at the guys turning and coming towards me. *Bring it fucker.*

I'm known for my speed, and this guy coming after me was going to be a challenge, but I needed it. I needed to feel alive again.

"Don't!" I heard Casey yell, but totally ignored her. I knew I could take him if I was smart.

He swung with this right hand, but missed, sending him off balance. Taking advantage, I laced my fingers together creating a large fist. Pulling back, I swung hard, hitting him directly in the back, making him fall to the ground on his knees. He grunted, and I was pleased with my skill. Swinging my right leg, my boot slammed his face hard, sending blood flying through the air. He fell with a thud.

Looking around the shop, I noticed the other guys were starting to come at me. I smiled. I loved this shit. It was so different fighting on my own turf than in jail.

"Please stop," Casey said, looking at her nails as if she were bored out of her mind.

"You could help me out here; ya know," I said, laughing.

Her eyes met mine. "You got this, and I just got a manicure while you were getting your hair done. I never get my nails done. I want to keep them nice, and I have to work with them." Casey smiled that beautiful smile.

Hearing boot steps behind me, I glanced quickly to see another man trying to sneak up on me. I loved the ones that thought they could one up me. When the guy approached, I turned quickly, kicking my leg up high and swung hard, hitting him directly in the face.

My joy was quickly tarnished when a gun was pressed into the back of my head and cocked. Shit. Well, this was how we were gonna play this, huh?

"Sugar, you just stirred up a shit storm." The southern drawl to his voice mixed with the smell of leather, cigarettes, and radiating testosterone would have made my pussy clench, but he ruined that by pressing a damn gun to my head.

"Low, don't." I ignored Casey just as I always did. Quickly, I turned my body. As my arm reached back to knock the gun out of his hand, I instantly froze. The three patch rag falling on his chest was a red light flashing in my eyes. Immediately, I stopped, putting my hands in front of me. I would never touch a brother, outside of the ring that is.

The man standing in front of me caught my breath and short-circuited my senses. His broad shoulders were covered with a skin-tight; black t-shirt and leather rag adorned with several patches that fit him like a glove. His bulging arms were covered in tattoos from the wrist up. They were flexed; one pointed the gun with precision, and the other was fisted at his side. His light caramel hair was cut short on the sides, but longer on the top, begging for a woman's fingers to run through it. His beard was cut very short to his skin making my mouth water, wondering what it would feel like between my thighs. His sapphire eyes narrowed at me as I stared effortlessly into them, becoming entranced unable to speak.

"What the fuck is going on here?" Breaking from this man's stare, I focused on the familiar voice I've missed for too long. Pops eyes swept the room quickly, and when his eyes landed on mine, the anger in them instantly faded. "What the hell's going on?" He eyed the man with the gun pointed directly at my head, and he clenched his hands into fists.

"Hey, Pops," I said, turning my eyes back to the beautiful specimen in front of me, wanting him to know that I wasn't afraid. If I needed a bullet in my head, so be it. I wouldn't shy away.

"You know this bitch?" the hot asshole in front of me clipped, and my lip curled slowly. If he wasn't wearing that rag, I'd show him how much of a bitch I could be.

"Put the damn gun down, Cruz," Pops said jokingly. The anger dripping off this man's face in front of me told me he didn't see anything funny about this. He began to take a step closer. "Cruz. Stop!" Pops barked loudly as the other guys started walking up behind him. Cruz instantly stopped but kept the gun on me. "Cruz, this is my daughter, Princess."

"Shit. Are you fucking kidding me?" Cruz's anger was actually pretty funny, and I had to stifle the small laugh that wanted to escape. I had too much respect to let it fly. But the shocked look on his face was pretty priceless coming from a tattooed hot-ass. I probably should have told him that sooner, but what can I say... I was born a bitch.

"No, I'm not fucking kidding you. Get the fuck away from her, and put the goddamn gun down." Turning my head towards Pops, I could see he was fuming. Whenever Pops was mad, his forehead turned bright red, and the lines throughout it became more prominent along with the vein in his neck that ticked with his heartbeat. It's a look I always hated growing up; it used to scare the ever-loving shit out of me.

My eyes flicked back while Cruz took one more look at me. "If you're still pissed later, we can meet in the ring." I smiled my damnedest. I could see the smoke threatening to come out of his ears. Confusion laced his eyes, but I wasn't about to explain right now. I held out my hand to Cruz, "Nice to meet ya. I'm Harlow." He stared me down as if he was hoping he could make me combust into a million pieces. Sorry Buddy, your super powers, won't work. I've been here too long to let that get me.

He tentatively lowered the gun, putting it behind his back, bringing his hand to mine. My hand slipped into his warm, rough, strong grip, a shock raced through my body, beginning at our connected hands and racing all the way through to my feet setting my body on fire. "Cruz." Snapping myself out, I pulled out of his grasp quickly not wanting him to feel the same. Breaking away from his intense eyes, I winked, brushing past him, I jumped in my Pops' arms. He picked me up and hugged me tight.

"Hi Daddy," I whispered in his ear, so he was the only one who could hear. I hadn't called him that in public since I was a kid. He's Pops to everyone around here, including me.

"Hey, Baby Girl. About time you got back here." He squeezed me and set me down on my feet. Looking up at him, his long black beard had a lot of gray growing through it, making it look salt and pepperish. The hair on his head looked the same, but with even grayer hairs sprinkled throughout. The eyes I stared into were the most beautiful powder blue. They were the eyes that held safety for me through all of these years. Sporting a lot more lines around his eyes, I wondered how he's been feeling.

"You okay, Pops?" I asked, tilting my head to the side and raising my eyebrows. My hands rested on his chest.

"I am now." His beard tried to hide his smile, but I saw it there, his silver front tooth flashing at me, the smile warmed me like no other. My Pops may not lead a conventional life, but one thing was an absolute; he loved his family and would do anything for us.

"You come back, and I get nothing?" Turning towards the low voice, I launched myself into my brother's arms, wrapping my arms around him as tight as I possibly could, squeezing the shit out of him. My brother... and this one was by blood. Growing up, we knew he'd be a member of the club as soon as he could be patched in. We were raised here together. Ma kept me further away than G.T., but that was for obvious reasons. G.T. patched in when he turned eighteen. I was so damn proud of him.

"Hi, G.T.," I said, burrowing myself in his strong chest.

"Hey, girl. You doin' all right?" He was utterly handsome. His short beard covered his face, while his blonde-brown hair hung low to his shoulders. He had the exact same navy eyes that I had, and every time I looked into them, I felt that same deep connection we've had since we were kids. I would do anything for him, and I knew he would for me. His tatted up arms were rock solid, and the shirt he was wearing was tight around the sleeves, showing every ripple. His small nose and strong jaw complete the package. Not that I was attracted to him, but the hordes of women that came and went for him definitely were.

"Yeah, Baby Brother. I'm good." I smiled up at him, turning to see all the men that I've known my entire life. Pride and joy melted through my heart. After hugging Dagger, Rhys, Zed, and Becs, I looked for him. Our President. I know I'm not a member, but I am in this family, and Diamond was our head man.

"Where's Diamond?" I asked Pops, looking behind him at the strong men I've grown up caring about. Yes, they were menacing, and no one would want to piss them off, but to me, they were my family. I loved each of them in their own way.

"He's inside. We wanted to check out everything before having him come out." Diamond was king around here. We all respected him and accepted his words as law. He took over as President after my Gramps passed away with Pops as his Vice President. He was sharp as a tack and knew his shit. He's a very smart business man and rode with the guys regularly. You'd never know he was pushing seventy.

"I'll see him in a minute. I need to see Sting." I needed him more than I needed to breathe at the moment.

"Come on." G.T. put his arm around my shoulders squeezing me as he led me to the back room.

Blocking the path in front of us was the garage man from earlier. "I'm so sorry. I was just trying to protect him." His voice was shaky, but who could blame him, I dislocated his nose.

"I appreciate that. Thanks." I smiled sweetly. I knew he was just doing his job. I just didn't care, 'cause no one keeps me away from my man. Could I have handled it differently, sure, but shit happens.

G.T. opened the door, and sitting inside was my man. In the middle of the room, my '97 Ultra Groundpounder Hardtail stood proudly. His chrome body hard and the beautiful red and black paint graced him like a glove. He was the ultimate man. He felt great between my legs, never let me down, and was always there when I was in need. Warmth and love flowed through my body.

"Anyone been taking him out?" I asked to the roomful of men that piled in behind us.

"I have. He's in good shape." Pops' voice came from behind. I knew could count on him.

"Thanks, Pops," I said straddling my beast

between my thighs. Reaching for the handlebars, I fired him up. The roar of the engine and the rough vibrations had my panties growing instantly wet. They didn't call this machine a Milwaukee vibrator for nothing.

"Umm… You okay, Princess?" G.T. asked eyeing me, a wide grin spread across my face. "I'm not gonna sit here and watch you get off."

Looking up at him, I responded, "Then you better get the hell out of here quick." My body was burning for release. It'd been way too long, and the vibrations were just too damn good hitting my clit just perfectly.

"I'll watch." Dagger cut through, crossing his arms across his chest.

"Dagger, you'd stop to watch two dogs fuck," I said, wiggling my eyebrows suggestively.

"Damn right, and the only thing better than watching you come would be my dick making you do it." Dagger's been in the club for years and was a monumental whore who fucked anything that had a hole, female of course, and made no qualms about it, even to his ol' lady. Dagger's a very rugged man. His leathery skin was masked by his long blond hair that's braided down his back with his red, white and blue bandana covering across his forehead. He's made no secret over the years that he'd love to take me for a ride. Too bad for him, I stay far away from brothers.

"You're not watching my girl. Get the fuck out!" Pops barked at the men, but none of them seemed to move, surprising me. G.T. and Pops made a quick exit. I shook my head, swallowing my laughter.

Getting back to the task at hand, I felt my body almost there. My hips rubbed back and forth on the seat, feeling my strong man taking care of me. Closing my eyes, the hot rush of feelings took over while I continued rocking back and forth. I didn't give two shits if the guys were there. I've seen them do more garbage in that clubhouse than I'd care to mention.

Sparks flew through my body, and my breath became sparse. Throwing my head back, I enjoyed the feelings racing through my body. Damn, I loved my man. Opening my eyes, every eye in the room was staring at me, and I couldn't help the amusement coursing through me. I shut down Sting and pulled myself off of him, feeling my damp panties rubbing against my jeans, making me smile. I needed to take him out for a ride very soon.

"Damn girl."

The story continues in Ravage Me (Ravage MC#1)
out now! http://amzn.to/1R66ohV
www.authorryanmichele.net
http://www.facebook.com/AuthorRyanMichele
http://www.twitter.com/Ryan_Michele